Cargo Trouble

Nicky Penttila

Wondrous Publishing

Copyright © 2023 by Nicky Penttila

ISBN 979-8-854762-07-6

All rights reserved. No portion of this book may be reproduced in any form without written permission from the publisher or author, except as permitted by U.S. copyright law.

The story, all names, characters, and incidents portrayed are fictitious. No identification with actual persons (living or deceased), places, buildings, and products is intended or should be inferred.

Book Cover by John A. Spillane

Illustrations by Envato

First edition 2023

Cargo Trouble

Chapter One

The snake, apparently, had conveyed with the ship.

Frankie stumbled upon Little Minnie as the pale giant reptile was recharging—basking, if another snake were doing it—under the grow lights in the starship's garden room. She'd come in for a sprig of mint, but that thought vanished under the weight of her surprise. She slowly knelt by the long, soft nest that had seen better days. Old Peters had made Minnie a new nest but she hadn't taken to it, so now that one was serving as a cushion up in the rec space. Old Peters had been fond of cushions, and most of those had conveyed, as well.

But they didn't need care and feeding.

One of Minnie's eyes was partly open, but looked as if it wanted to be closed. Frankie wasn't sure how an eye could communicate like that, but didn't question it. She respected Minnie's boundaries. As she stepped out of the room, the door whooshing shut, she started the call to Old Peters. While waiting, she squatted down to see if she could see any snake prints on the extra button panel by the jamb. Minnie knew how to press these to gain entry to places all over the ship; how long that had taken to teach her, Frankie couldn't even guess.

"Frankie!" The voice was a warm scratch on an unacknowledged itch. "Miss me already? How's the Spear?"

"Spherical as always." Why the bulbous cargo ship had such a sharp name was yet another mystery. Frankie wasn't about to spend the time or the credits to rename her, though, so Spear she would remain. "One question, though. Didn't you forget somebody?"

A pause at the other end. "Oh, you mean Minnie. No, girl, she's yours. She'd never leave the Spear, her bones wouldn't take it. We're both at the ends of our useful lives now."

Frankie rolled her eyes. Despite his nickname, Peters wasn't so old. Sure, he had serious mobility issues from the wars, but the ship was modified to help with that. He had retired because he could afford to.

Lucky for her, since that meant she could afford the awfully reasonable price he'd named for the ship. "You're sure? Isn't Stackfield low-grav?"

"Don't think my new neighbors would be too hot on a snake that was taller than they are. And she'd find precious few little mousies scuttling down here."

"She is good for the ship, yes," Frankie said. "But seriously, she's going to miss you terribly." Frankie and Minnie were on live-and-let-live terms, not really cuddle buddies the way Minnie and Peters were. And Minnie could be moody, and hide when feeling low.

"She'll be fine. You will, too. Gotta go—it's time for my waterdance class. My friend who got me this place says it's like happy hour for us geezers."

Frankie blinked at the idea of Peters in a waterdance class, and then remembered to blink the call off. Her stomach rumbled. Mint, for the porridge with the weird smell. She tapped the lower

Cargo Trouble

open-door panel with her foot, whispered an apology to Minnie, grabbed a sprig, and took it back to the kitchen. While heating up the porridge, she opened her shopping list for when they got to Rosing Station and added frozen mice.

There was always a chance that the cargos of grains and other foodstuffs the Spear transported wouldn't attract mice or other invasive critters this run.

But it hadn't happened yet.

No problems at Rosing Station. Frankie had seconded to Old Peters for two full cycles before taking the Spear out on her own, so she knew all the port stewards and how to get around. The Spear had a portering contract for organic materials needing fast shipping to the inner ring of planets in the system. It was a steady job and usually took up only part of the cargo space, so she could freelance cargo for extra credits.

Rosing Station, the biggest and newest in this system, sat in the Lagrange Point between two top-producing agricultural planets. Frankie always picked up seed here for the less-blessed worlds on the route. Seed packed tight, so half the hold was free for extras. Frankie had drained her account buying the Spear outright, and needed to rebuild her safety net. And to buy some insurance, at least collision.

She sauntered into the economy section of the station's lower ring, looking for the ramen shop she remembered. She liked sauntering, that saucy sway of the hips. It made her feel captainlike, not like what she used to be.

The section, two stories high with a narrow bridge-deck all around, hummed and burbled; people of all sorts walking and talking, haggling, slurping noodles. The noodles here were stellar, of course, so close to the source.

She stopped at a specialty grocery, noisy with birds and people shouting. She checked out all the types of mice before making her order. She'd forgotten to ask Peters how much Minnie needed to eat, so she ordered fifty. That must be enough, for one haul.

With her short hair a new red, and her identity not triggering to anyone here at the edge of Cooperative space, Frankie felt free to roam. The people who needed to know where she was knew it; everybody else could find themselves stuck in a broken airlock.

The shop was still there, the noodles still delicious. So much better than porridge. She was on her second bowl and thinking about asking the proprietor if they sold freeze-dried servings when her message light blinked.

A local call.

She did not panic. She did not answer the call.

She slowly slurped her noodles, savoring fresh coriander and chilis. It was probably someone wanting something shipped. Speed-of-light response to her open-cargo posting, though. Maybe they were desperate. So let them stew, and they might not notice if she boosted the standard fee.

She had many options, and the best one was the ability to say no.

Chapter Two

"No," she said.

The message had been from Skoll Shipping, the biggest cargo hauler in the sector. Proudly family-owned: Two younger Skolls sat across from her, taking up all the space in the small booth in a nondescript cafe in the inner ring of third section. Even seated, they were tall, and wide, and a shade of gray that indicated a once-darker complexion that had been in space too long.

Frankie was short and squat in comparison—planet-raised. Her skin was only starting to take on that sheen, and even just a week on-planet would wash it away. A lot of rich spacers used the sun booths to look planet-raised. The Skolls proudly did not.

They also did not eat or drink in front of people, which made meeting in a cafe less than comfortable.

Peters had told her to steer clear of the Skolls. They held most of the portering contracts in this sector, for the big hauls. She was just a little fish. She should be beneath their notice.

"It's a reasonable offer," the one in the green sari said. They hadn't introduced themselves, so she wasn't sure what the hierarchy was. Neither talked much, probably taking advantage of their prey's nerves.

Well, she wasn't prey. She took a sip of her real-bean coffee and savored it. Matcha was fine for everyday, but sometimes you just wanted a rich, thick blend to savor. When someone else was paying. She held the small saucer a shade longer, breathing in the steamy goodness.

"We're not in competition. I don't see why you need the Spear."

"We don't need the Spear. Only the contract."

"You're a new captain," said the one in gold and blue. "This route will go dull for you in no time."

"You're right, I'm new. So how about we postpone this conversation for a rotation and see how it goes?"

The one in green crossed their beautifully bangled arms. "We thought we had a deal with Old Peters."

Frankie tried to hide her surprise, and probably failed. What deal?

"Then you came along," blue sari said, "and we didn't hear from Peters again."

Frankie took another sip, larger, draining the saucer. This was trouble, and she didn't want to leave any coffee behind if she had to run.

She set it down, keeping her hands on it to capture the last of its warmth. "Captain Peters swore there was no other claim to the Spear when we registered the sale."

Green sari sighed, looking toward the service counter. Must be tough to smell all the delicious pastries and know you can't eat any of them. Too bad.

Blue sari set their clasped hands on the table and stared steadily at Frankie. "You don't know how it is around here, I see that. Here on the edges, we do a lot of things that aren't exactly by the book, if you know what I mean. There's agreements, and then there's agreements. And there's tradition, and precedent."

That was plain confusing. "Tradition?" she said tentatively.

"Exactly. Skoll Shipping traditionally"—hard emphasis on that word—"has right of first offer for all cargo transport from this station."

"Ah," Frankie said. "Peters should have offered. And you would have turned it down, because it is such a small contract, compared to the loads you haul. And we would be in the same position."

"We would not be in the same position. We would have purchased the contract. And for more than you did." They opened their hands like giving up an offering. "We offer the same price to you we would have to Old Peters. An immediate profit."

Now Frankie crossed her arms. She had spent two years setting this up. Learning the ropes, getting comfortable with a lot of quiet time and a giant snake. She needed something to do—something far away from everybody else—and this was ideal.

But she didn't want to be owned. Even if Skoll would keep her and the Spear on, and they would have to, for a cycle at least, she would not be in control of her life. Again.

"No," she said. "Thank you."

The one in green hissed in a breath. But the one in blue held up a hand, stalling them. "I understand you need to stay distant from the capital."

The one in green couldn't hold it in. "We know who you are."

Frankie went still. It wasn't a secret, of course. She just didn't want to be paraded around anymore. She didn't want to be known as a Child Orphan of Wala one second longer.

That life, traveling Co-op space collecting pity and uncomfortable pauses, was another kind of death. Let Beth keep doing it; she liked it. Frankie was out.

But she wasn't above using it for her own benefit. "You would take advantage of someone who's already lost so much?"

Blue sari sat unruffled, like an auntie who brings you sweets and then swipes them off the table to eat herself when you're not looking. "It's a good deal. You should take it."

"Thank you, no. If that's it, then?" Frankie stood up.

The two Skolls also rose, faster than she'd expected. The one in green loomed over the table, over her. "Take the deal."

Frankie nodded her head in farewell. "Safe travels," she said.

They did not give the familiar response back. They said nothing at all.

Bullies, plain and simple. They had no power over her.

Chapter Three

Frankie was barely through the airlock and into the dock where Spear was tethered when she heard the argument.

The voices, one high, one low, and one screeching, were three or four slips down the pier, so they must be really loud. Even with only their stern tied to the dock, most haulers were huge. Just to walk to her slip from the last station airlock would take most of an hour. Frankie looked longingly at the little red miniwagon floating beside her. She could have ridden it to her ship, except it was full of spare parts, boxed ramen, and a bag of dead mice.

It would be good for her to walk, and the dock was lovely, for a dock. The pale gray ceiling so far away you couldn't even see the rivets gave her all the space she wanted. The gigantic outer portals in the distance promised adventure. The constant rattling and banging of folks getting their ships spaceworthy sang in her ears.

But the argument sounded a sour note.

Frankie dawdled, hoping they would finish whatever their discussion was, but even at half-speed she came upon them mid-battle. The captain of the ship, a boxy hauler, stood blocking the entrance to the cargo ramp, a true-to-life parrot on his shoulder. The parrot seemed to have much to squawk at an amazingly blond person draped in multicolored silks. This person was gesticulating wildly at the stoic shipper, and then at the shipping box twice their height that filled the entire width of the pier.

Frankie would have to shimmy to get past that behemoth box. Her miniwagon needed a floor to hover above; if the shimmy space was too narrow, the wagon might plunge to the port floor, far, far below.

No way that cargo should be here. There were rules about moving cargo, the chief one being always keep it flowing. Never block the route.

Now she was mad at the all-colors person, too. She didn't even wait for a pause in the overloud conversation to shout, "Excuse me."

The shipper was the captain, a friend of Old Peter. Punter couldn't be his name, but it was the only thing she knew him by. Maybe it was the bird's name? He nodded to her.

The stranger spun on a heel and glared at her, but stopped talking. He was one of the pretty ones, who probably never had a major problem in their lives. No wonder he was overreacting to whatever was wrong.

"Are you going to move this box?" she said. "People need to get by."

"I'm trying," he stretched out the word. "But my good man here refuses to honor our contract."

"The contract says pay up-front." The captain spread out his hands. The bird spread its wings behind him. "I'm waiting."

Typical. It was only a few days until the new month. Sir Pretty had probably blown through his allowance.

"I told you, good sir, that the funds are at the destination. Here, the proof." He flicked at something on his wristcom.

Cargo Trouble

The captain did not look at his comm, or at the tablet in his hand that probably held the ship's manifest. "And I told you, it needs to be here, with me."

This argument would not end soon. Frankie nodded to the captain and started toward the box. How narrow was that shimmy going to have to be?

"Wait!" The colorful person approached her. She stopped her wagon, again. "Perhaps you could assist me where this captain will not."

He had a beautiful face. Big dark eyes like a cartoon character. Wide mouth that surely needed to smile a lot. Clear brow crowned by perfectly cared-for waves of hair in all colors of blond. The one piece of jewelry he wore was a pendant—black onyx?—that signaled masculine gender while looking rather feminine.

A player.

She jammed her hands in the back pockets of her tunic. She'd forgotten there was a dead mouse in the right pocket, thawing for Minnie. At least it was in a wrapper.

"Sir. The captain is a wise man. If he finds fault with your contract, I believe I would find the same fault." She was not going to extend a player any credit.

"Oh! He is so unreasonable. We've shipped many, many times with him, and he knows we're always good for it."

The captain snorted. "After months of dunning."

Something smelled ... odd. Frankie frowned and took another whiff. Organic, but not the right kind of organic. Not exactly rotten, but something.

"See. She smells it too. There's something wrong with your box."

"There's nothing wrong with my box. It's carrying organics. It's going to have an organic smell." He fiddled with his wristcom, a fancy model with a gorgeous black band "It's cleared all customs, see? There is no problem."

The captain shook his head. "No credits, no portering. No problem." He turned and stomped up the ramp.

At least the argument was done. Frankie powered up the mini-wagon again and stepped toward the edge of the dock. She wished she had a safety line, but who could have known one was needed in port?

"Captain, please, a moment. Please."

She sighed and turned back to the annoyance. She wished, again, that her parents had not trained her to be polite to all people.

"I'm Morgan, uh, Cloud. Morgan Cloud. It's very nice to meet you, captain?"

"Styles."

"Captain Styles. You're new here?" He leaned against his box as if they were having a conversation in a shopping court, not blocking the entire pier. "I haven't seen you around."

Frankie had no time for this, whatever it was, flirting? "We're done."

"No, wait. I know a way you won't have to risk your life trying to get around this box." A sound came from the top of the box, a shuffling. Three dock crewmembers peered over on the edge. The player stepped out of the way as they lowered themselves down to the dock. The dock's cat, a massive, scraggly, lumpy thing, remained on the top edge, eyeing the parrot.

"You could ship it."

As if. "For free? I don't think so." She put her hands on her hips.

"Of course not. I have the credits. I'll show you." He looked her up and down. "You look hungry. How about I buy you dinner and we can talk about it?"

"Not hungry. Not interested."

Cargo Trouble

He looked over the contents of the miniwagon. "I know a great ramen shop up on the top tier. Noodles to die for. And the dining room has a view of the big park, too."

Frankie paused. "Peppermint ice cream?"

Morgan considered. "Not there. But nearby."

It wouldn't work. But, a free meal?

"You won't stiff me?"

"Me?" He held a hand in front of where his heart should be. "Never."

She could eat on his credits. And there must be a good story about this smelly box.

"I need to drop off my supplies. Meet you there?"

"Excellent! How about I give you a hand up?" He saw her confusion and pointed to the top of the box. "Like those good service workers."

Frankie scoped the jump. Might be done. Morgan must have seen her approval. He backed up to the box, bent his knees, clasped his hands, and held them out to her.

She set a foot on his hands and a hand on the box as high as she could reach. He stood and pushed. Easy scramble. On top, the smell was stronger. It reminded her of a visit to the country when she was little.

Frankie reset the miniwagon to float higher. It rose halfway, but started to struggle. In the end, Morgan gave it a boost, too.

"Perfect," he said. "See you in an hour?"

Chapter Four

Frankie had changed her mind in the time it took to stow the supplies. Minnie snubbed her nose at the mouse but then looked affronted when Frankie started to go without leaving it behind. So now there was maybe a dead mouse carcass in the greenroom.

Another prima donna. She only needed one. Less than one.

She should call this meeting off. Pick up some farm implements or something simple like that. No more organics. What if they infected the seed? Sure, the containers were supposed to prevent that, but if mice could find a way surely some virus or whatever could.

She got the ping from "Morgan" with coordinates to the shop, which she'd never heard of. The reviews were stellar.

She couldn't be always saying no. The sad echoes in her empty credit accounts were forever clanging in her thoughts. Just do the shipping, get it over with. Clear the nagging worries out of her head.

She changed out of her everyday and into the navy tunic that

Beth said made her skin glow—at least when she had planet tan—and soft boots that matched her leggings. Her hair was fine. She reminded herself: Peppermint ice cream.

Someone had shoved Morgan's cargo so the longer side ran along the walkway, opening a third of it up to travel again. As she passed it, she tried to place the smell, but nothing reasonable came to mind. Nobody needed to transport milorganite—people made waste on every planet.

The trip up to the third ring was a parade of fashion. Economy featured sturdy fabrics in bright colors. At second ring, the elevator doors opened to a sea of muted colors and smoothed-down hair and clothing. At third ring, she stepped out into a smaller crowd with louder taste: asymmetric cuts, hard and soft fabrics, colors that changed. And a lot of wrinkling; she felt tempted to bunch up her tunic to match the style. The fabric was rich enough to pass, barely. She was glad she hadn't worn the tan one.

There wasn't much anyone could do about the architecture of the station. Each ring was built the same, triple-contained space worthy. So the main difference walking the shopping courts here was the ornament on the same five styles of boxed-into-the-wall stores and freestanding carts. But they really did it up here: Each shop had a subtle scent, all of them alluring to humans, apparently. Frankie found herself at the threshold of a high-fashion store before she realized it. Only the shocked affront on the face of the human assistant inside brought her to her senses.

The restaurant did not look like a noodle shop. The wall facing the walk glowed amber. If she didn't know better, she would have thought it was solid amber. Light from inside seemed to highlight fossils in the wall. What a marvelous illusion.

And expensive.

Morgan wasn't waiting inside the restaurant. He lounged against the faux-amber, his multicolored tunic alternately matching and clashing with the wall behind him. His multi-hued hair, which did not change, fit perfectly in the setting. He was messing up his pretty face by scowling at his tablet. As soon as he saw her, he slid the tablet into his pocket.

"Captain. You're such a restful sight. No, seriously—I mean that in a good way."

"Mr. Cloud. You look well." That seemed safe enough to say.

"If you like, I can turn off my tunic for dinner, so you don't have to watch me swirl. One more thing." He reached for her, maybe to take her arm.

Frankie jumped back.

"Sorry, sorry. This isn't starting well, is it?" He smiled, a soft thing that somehow communicated regret, warmth, and calculation. "This is the thing: I know the proprietor here, Stella. We're friends. I helped design this wall, in fact." He waved toward the amber.

Frankie could not help herself. "It's astounding."

"Five-scan illusion, yeah. Anyway, Stella is prickly about how people order their meals. If it's all right with you, I will order for both of us."

Frankie crossed her arms. "You think I don't know how to order in a high Co-op restaurant?"

"Do you?" He obviously thought not.

Frankie did. She'd been partly raised under the supervision of the regent of the Co-op herself. But it wouldn't do to let that out, if she wanted to remain merely a captain here. She would need to make mistakes with all the glasses and implements, too, to keep the false front.

This was why she didn't like to be with people. They just kept pushing at her jammed doors.

"No," she said. She wasn't that hungry, anyway. "Let's just go get some ice cream."

The relief on Morgan's face was fleeting but obvious. He probably didn't have the credits. That's why he was taking her to a friend's restaurant. It wasn't to impress her—he probably thought she didn't know enough about fine dining to be impressed.

Fancy-pants player.

Morgan also sauntered, but he had to slow it down so much to stay even with her short legs that his gait looked like he was walking through water. The ice cream place was apparently back toward the elevator she'd come up in. How had she not noticed it? Morgan directed her toward a short alley between buildings. He did not try to touch her.

She gasped. There was a park back here!

A narrow strip of green ran behind all the buildings on this side of the ring. Small plants and flowery bushes flowed down the strip, with benches and soft ground seating sprinkled about.

"Pretty great, huh? All the restaurants are on this side, so they can take advantage of the view." Morgan turned right, and she could see the snack kiosk right away. The sweet and spicy scents of the blooms filled the air. It really did smell good up here.

Morgan did have the credits to obtain a crunchy saucer of peppermint ice cream and another of plain chocolate. They sat at one of the ground-cushions, side by side, and dove in. Frankie turned a little away from Morgan so his swirling clothes wouldn't distract her.

Bliss. Smooth and creamy, sharp and tangy. After the second spoonful, she sighed and lowered the saucer. She needed time to savor.

The last time she'd had peppermint was—what?—twenty years ago. Her eighth birthday.

Her last on Wala.

Peppermint was considered a weed among most of the Co-op

planets. It was pretty invasive, but could be tamed by using pots. Old Peters hadn't wanted it in his greenroom.

But it was her greenroom now.

Morgan seemed to consider her pause in eating an opportunity for conversation. "So. My cargo. It must be at Smithson Station in ten days. Earlier is better."

Frankie frowned, and then took another spoonful of ice cream. Letting it melt on her tongue, its sweet tang rolling through her sinuses, she had to admit: She was not always free to say no. Being a businessperson meant making deals whenever they came up, melting ice cream or no.

"Show me the manifest," she said.

It was on the surface of his tablet immediately. His hands were free—somehow, he'd finished all his ice cream already and was chewing on the hard-cookie spoon.

So *that* was the smell. She did remember it, from visiting farms near her grandparents.

"That whole big box for only two horses?"

"Racehorses," he said, pride in his voice. "It's a whole stable, with space for months of fodder and a self-contained reclamation system. A veterinary setup for minor injuries. Plus capsule space for the jockey to sleep, when it's settled at the track."

She had to stare at him. "You ship racehorses off-planet?" The cost of doing such a thing was astronomical. He wasn't a player. He was insane.

He grinned at her. "Eat up. These aren't merely racehorses, captain. They are winners. My family has raised horses for generations." He shrugged. "They move where we move."

"And you're moving to Smithson Station?" It was an older station—only two levels—but it was on her route. Old Peters's Stackfield Base was nearby.

"Gods, no." Morgan actually shuddered, which set his tunic

into hurricane mode. Frankie hastily looked away. When she looked back, he'd done something to it; now it was nonmoving swirls of red, pink, and white. "That's where all the horses are going. They have to be there for a week before the race, so everyone can see there's no doping and all that. Then they'll join me down on Hondichi, where the track is."

Somehow, all her ice cream had vanished. She lifted the saucer, eyeing between its waffles for even a bit more. "You think they've run out of peppermint?" she said.

He chuckled, a honeyed sound, and reached for her saucer. She handed it to him and sat back, leaning on her hands, as he went to get her more. The curve of the outer ring up here even had portholes, regularly spaced at adult chest height. What a job that would be to make sure none of them leaked.

"Okay," she said, after her first—second—initial hunger had been slaked. "But still, how is it economically feasible?

"It isn't, always. You need to place in the top three in a race and win some credits to cover the cost. If you win, or place in multiple races, that's when you make a profit. That's why most people bring two or more horses. Double the chances."

"And if you lose?" He seemed like someone who did not consider that he would lose.

"I have insurance. I have a contract to sell the pair: one price if one of them places, one price if they win, and a base price no matter what happens." He shrugged. "It's not even really a gamble: If we win, I win. If we place, I win. If we lose everything, I'm covered."

"And this base price. This gets paid up-front?"

"Exactly. As soon as we get there, and the horses pass inspection. There's your fee."

Frankie crunched on her saucer. She'd need to see this contract.

Cargo Trouble

She did not need to see the horses. That would bring up too many memories.

Did she trust this man? She had plenty of experience with fancy boys, and he didn't strike her as one of the mean ones. Or one of the hidden-mean ones.

"How much could you give me right now? As security."

He sighed. "Well. All the peppermint ice cream you can fit in your freezer?"

She had to laugh.

"Deal."

Morgan made one more push. "And might you take passengers, as well? I could bunk in a crew cabin, nothing fancy."

Frankie bristled. She was a businessperson now, sure, but she didn't need to sell all her space. It had taken her a while to warm to Old Peters, and he was the nicest they came. She wasn't ready.

"No. Not this trip," she said to soften it. "Don't you have a ship of your own?"

"Not exactly," he sighed. "But no worries, I'll find a way to meet you there. And the sale can go through, with or without me."

Morgan Cloud wasn't there for the loading of his box. The dockworkers wouldn't move it down to the Spear, but the parrot and its captain had departed earlier, so she hopped the Spear down to that slip and used her own drones to wrestle the thing aboard. As they were securing it, the dock's older undersupervisor came up the ramp, lingering in the doorway. Frankie enjoyed the inspector's sly sense of humor when she wasn't its target.

"Thank you for removing the impediment. Your ship is in the wrong slip."

"Thank you, chief assistant dockmaster. I'm ready to cast off."

"Do you have room for another small cargo? Also for Smithson Station. Double standard rate."

Frankie hadn't known you could pick up cargo on the fly like this. But it was the assistant dockmaster, so it had to be legit.

"Sure. What is it?"

"Adzuki, they tell me. A half-ton."

Beans? To an agriculture planet?

"Standard contract?" She saw it on her wristcom in seconds. Nothing out of the ordinary.

She signed the contract and sent it back. "More the merrier."

A half-hour later she had a portal time. An hour later she was off the dock and under way to Smithson Station.

Chapter Five

Minnie must have eaten the mouse. Frankie didn't see it or her lengthy friend in the greenroom. She flicked her wrist to show the ship's map. Captain's suite.

Where Frankie was headed anyway. The Spear could pilot herself, although Frankie had widened the parameters for when she needed to sound an alert. Old Peters had been more sanguine about those things than Frankie was. Maybe when she was Old Frankie, she'd ease up on the controls.

The captain's suite had three rooms: the center one for meetings, one to the left for sleeping and washing, one on the right for whatever else. The last room was bare: Peters had taken all his collections and musical instruments with him, and Frankie didn't have anything to put in its place. She'd always traveled light.

But now she did have the space, she wondered what to put in it. A game room? There already was one of those, up by the kitchen. Not a music room—her little guitar would look mighty lonely there, and she liked to play it in bed, anyway. Maybe a reading room?

For now, the room would stay empty. She walked through the office and into the bedroom, also rather severe at the moment. At least she had the navy and silver fuzzy blanket Beth had sent as a gift when she bought the Spear. "In your colors!" the note accompanying it read.

Minnie was here, draped along the top of her wardrobe. Her "stick"—more like a tree without branches or an overgrown coat rack—was still in the whatever room. Come to think of it, that should have tipped Frankie off that Minnie was still here.

But of course, Minnie wouldn't want to hang out in an empty room, so here she was. Frankie suspected there were still whiffs of Old Peters about here, to a sensitive nose.

"Okay, Minnie," she said. "We need to set some boundaries. This is my room now."

Her words did not move the snake, though it did give her a look, and a slow blink.

Well, if she was going to stay, it couldn't be on Frankie's dresser. The stick would have to come into the bedroom. Then later—or sooner—she would see if Minnie consented to having the stick in the office room.

Frankie had to summon the littlest hauler bot to help her even lift the thing. It helped a lot when it pointed out that the stick was bolted to the floor; Frankie had seen the bolts on the wall and thought the stick must spin when the gravity went out. Between them, they wrestled it into the bedroom close by the door and secured it with what she hoped were temporary, easily removable, bolts. Frankie thanked the bot and sent it on its way.

Almost immediately, Minnie dropped to the floor and launched herself onto her stick. She settled into the familiar loops Frankie remembered from evenings of music with Old Peters.

"I miss him, too," she said, resting a hand on one of the loops. Minnie's skin was dry and warm, comforting.

Cargo Trouble

Frankie changed into her comfy mid-space clothes: soft pants, long sleeved Galactic U T-shirt, a thick navy-and-silver cardigan with big buttons and pockets. She kept her grav-boots on. She'd learned that lesson hard.

Passing Minnie on the way out, she tried to remember: Weren't horses afraid of snakes?

The cat was in the kitchen.

The one from Rosing Station dock, with the perpetual just-shocked-looking fur. Striped, sort of—tufted, mostly—in grays and blacks. Its gaze was unusually steady. A solid, sturdy body, it looked too heavy to lift. Maybe it wasn't a cat? But it had the pointy ears, complete with black tufts on the tips.

It perched on the back of the three-sided nook-bench with the orange cushions, above the spot where Frankie usually had her breakfast. Actually, all her meals now that she was on her own.

Did the cat know that?

"Good morning," she said, assuming the cat was on Galactic Standard Time. The cat did not acknowledge her as she passed to the smaller galley to start the morning brew. Frankie reached for the cupboard for porridges, and then stopped. Her belly wasn't feeling it.

She sat on the bench across from her usual spot, facing the cat but with her back to the open doorway. Foolish choice, a long-gone security instructor whispered in her thoughts. Stand down, brain, it's safe here. She stared at the cat-thing. It stared back.

She blinked first. "How did you get here?" Okay, that was a dumb question. "You chased something, and got stuck, right? You better've caught it."

The cat—she was going to call it a cat—jumped down to the seat cushion, spun twice, and settled in a circle shape. It blinked at her.

"Great. Well, I hope you like frozen mice. It's at least a month till we can get you home."

It set its head on its paws and closed its eyes. Frankie sipped her caffeine and decided that she would skip the gruel this morning. Would she find some other creature, one by one, in every room on the ship? Could add up to a lot of mouths to feed.

She scanned the ship's log—no problems overnight. When her cup was empty, she clicked her wristcom to scan and stretched her arm across the table. Time to read the cat's chip and tell whoever cared for this chonk where it had gotten to.

Before she could get a reading—almost before the scan's beam could have touched it—the cat squawked. It vaulted off the cushion, under the table, and away. Only the light breeze of its movement past her shin indicated which direction it had gone. And the growl from outside the door.

She swiveled in the seat to look out the door. The cat was on the far side, close to the wall. "Stand down, fuzzy head. I'm just trying to find out who to call. You don't want your people to worry, do you?"

The door slid shut.

Rude.

It must have bumped the lower open-button. It should have taken two intentional pushes to close a door at remain-open setting, though.

Frankie opened her to-do list and added check kitchen slide button. Top of the list was the ever-delightful cleaning of the filters. She promised herself the last of the fresh ramen for a job well done. And tried not to think about how much fur that big-pawed stowaway could shed.

Chapter Six

After a long, dusty shift, Frankie was ready to play. She passed from the living/piloting sphere into the cargo hold, grabbed a hand-hold, and slid the second door shut. She waved the soft lights on. The vast space always reminded her of images from biology class, objects of various shapes and sizes growing out into the center from the smooth walls of the hull. Maybe a cross-section of an intestine? Except way, way drier.

She extended the retractable walkway/ladder across the diameter of the hold. No need to stow it; there was plenty of space on this trip. The port bots had done a good job, balancing the load and making sure all was secure. She clicked on her grav-boots and walked among the cargo.

Minnie was in here somewhere. Frankie checked her comm. Down a ways, by the somewhat-smaller containers. There, just below the walkway.

Frankie loved to watch Minnie swim in no-G. Most snakes tied themselves in knots, confused by the absence of their inner sense of place. Minnie's senses were modified to ease the stress. She swam through the air the way others swam in water, only the curves turned into spirals here. Minnie also liked the walkway, an extra object to rebound from in the center of the hold.

Sometimes, she sped around the space, ricocheting around corners and zooming from wall to wall. Today, she was taking her time, going from carton to carton, spinning like an otter sometimes, other times bouncing in great arcs like she was the path of a child's rubber ball. Must be getting familiar with all the cargo.

Frankie didn't smell anything besides the usual ozone and a vague mustiness. Soon it would be hard to smell anything in the chill. No cargo that needed warmth, so the heaters were off to offset the extra solar charge she was using to get to Smithson Station early. The hold would get colder and colder during the trip. Neither she nor Minnie could stay that long.

The bots had secured the horse stable container, which had its own heat pump, by itself at the far end of the hold. From the walkway, it looked vertical. Did horses adapt to no-G?

Most mice couldn't—they would spin and spin, until Minnie caught them right away. But a few strains could, due to random mutation. Minnie caught them later. The port could scan for and kill the smallest virus and bug, but had to be careful around live plants and larger animals. So, mice.

Frankie reached the far wall and clicked her grav-boots off. She held the railing and pivoted to set her boots on the wall, putting new boot-prints over the boot-prints already there. Minnie had been keeping her in sight. She knew what boots on the wall meant. The snake twined itself into a spring, holding onto one of the cargo handles near the center of the hold.

Frankie used the railing to push herself into her own version of a spring. She let go, kicked off the wall, and went flying. A moment later, Minnie pushed, and by the time Frankie was flying by, Minnie had reached her. Perfect timing: Frankie reached for

Cargo Trouble

Minnie's long middle, and pushed, so gently, downward. The snake ricocheted toward some cargo, while Frankie kept her trajectory but tumbled head over heels. The game was to be facing the door by the time she got to the entry wall.

She was facing the door, a ways above it and upside down, when she got there. She grabbed one of the safety lines tacked along the walls and spun to land on her shoulder. Hand over hand, down to the walkway. Brilliant.

She could only make the fly once at a time, because Minnie would try to do it again, too, and tire herself out too much. Once was enough—Frankie's shoulders had relaxed, her breathing was good, and she was smiling.

Frankie was savoring the last of the fresh noodles and staring at that dustmop of a cat who was again lounging in her spot in the nook when the call came in. Not even a message, an actual voice call, beyond expensive when mid-space.

Morgan.

"Styles. What's wrong?" She knew to keep it short.

"Yeah, this is Morgan. You know that. I mean, it says, right?" The strain in his voice could have cracked glass.

"Why are you calling? Where are you?"

"Funny thing about that, heh heh." The tension ratcheted. Frankie could picture his lean, handsome face, shiny with sweat. "I'm in a bit of a pickle."

"You're in trouble?"

"Not trouble, really. Well, yes." His breathing was ragged. He wasn't making any sense.

Frankie panicked. She didn't care about him, not really, but what would she do with his cargo? What did she know of horses?

The cat, watching her, stretched slowly. It walked around the bench seat and plopped itself down on her cushion, its shoulder on her thigh. Its shoulder had some heft to it.

Morgan blew out a long, loud breath. "Okay, it's like this. I'm here, in the stable."

"You're in the ship?" Frankie couldn't stop her voice from breaking. She thought she was safe here. Her own ship.

Without thinking, she set her hand on the cat's flank. "Get out," she said. "No, I mean, what is the deal?"

"Okay, okay, I know you're mad, probably. There was sort of a problem with my berth on the passenger ship, and I had to get to Smithson, and there is space here for the jockey to travel with the horses, if necessary. So I took it."

Frankie scowled. Under her palm, the cat rumbled softly. "You didn't have the credits for transit. You stowed away. On my ship."

"You're cleared for passenger transit. I checked."

He hadn't checked. This call wasn't costing him anything.

What a prince.

"Well, thanks for telling me. See you at the station."

"No, don't hang up! Please. Please, I need your help." If anything, he sounded worse now. "Thing is, capsule berths trigger my claustrophobia. It's not long enough, for one, and I have to pretzel myself just to get in."

"You're afraid of enclosed spaces?"

"I thought I was over it. Look, I'm climbing the walls. I'm heaving, and my chest feels like it's going to burst. I'm scaring the horses, and they need to stay calm to pass inspection."

Just his description made Frankie's heart speed up. But what did it have to do with her?

"You know you're okay, right?"

"That is so not helping."

Cargo Trouble

"Fine. How about, get out, roam the cargo hold. Plenty of space there, and good air. It's cold, so bundle up."

A pause. "I was hoping I could come inside?"

"No."

"Just for a little bit? Until I calm down."

Frankie's last wonderful noodles had gone cold. This was her space. She already had unexpected roommates, first Minnie and now this cat whose name she didn't even know. That was enough.

But she also knew the blinding terror of panic attacks. She did not wish them even on her enemies—well, except maybe one of them. This thoughtless man, with his colors and his betting and his all the rest of it, was suffering. He did not know how large a gift he was asking for.

"Captain?" The voice a soft, sad peep.

"Fine." Frankie clenched her hand in the raggedy-soft fur of the stowaway next to her. "I'll meet you at the airlock."

Chapter Seven

"I brought gifts." Morgan slid out of the hold, landing neatly on his feet, a duffel bag in one hand and another cross-strapped to his torso. His hair did not gleam, his face did not glow. His hands shook. If Frankie hadn't seen him days ago at Rosings, she would have thought he had a terminal illness.

She was going to have to let him stay.

"Give me that." She reached for the bag in his hand. "Tough enough getting used to gravity again." As she took the bag from him, he grasped her wrist, briefly.

"Seriously. Thank you."

She shrugged it off. "I'm absolutely going to scan your cargo now, contract or no. No more stowaways."

He followed her up the spiral ladder and onto the main floor of the ship's middle segment, only huffing a little. "Actually, the stable has its own gravity."

She stopped mid-stride, turning back to him. "What?"

His head bumped her elbow, and he had to grab for the railing to steady his teeter. "Yeah. I didn't tell you?"

"You know you didn't." Micro-grav systems were known to overheat. And explode. As cargo, they were a must-declare.

"I forgot," he said. "Honest. We're always hauling it around. Never a problem." He did not look contrite. Probably considered it the least of his deceptions. "Anyway, it's freezing in the hold. Nothing's going to overheat in there."

Frankie sighed and stepped the rest of the way up. "No more surprises. Okay?"

He made a big deal of resting on the landing, hands on knees. Marking time. There were more surprises to come, she was sure of it.

"How about this?" he finally said. "You agree not to look me up on the nets, and I'll agree not to look you up." He spread his hands. "Then, no surprises."

"I have nothing to hide," she said, and stopped.

A corner of his mouth pulled up. "A young, obviously university educated, perfect High Galactic speaker, piloting a cargo ship on a backwater route. Nothing to hide?"

He had her. What hay he could make with her checkered history. "Fine. Agreed. What did you bring me?"

"Show me the way to the mess hall, and I'll tell you."

On this floor, two pairs of crew cabins faced each other. She'd stow him in the one across the hall, farthest from her. She didn't look forward to keeping her doors closed, but so it would be.

As she stepped through the inner airlock, she heard that cabin door whoosh shut. Another panel-break? She bumped the floor panel to open the door, stepped in, and looked around. Nothing weird in the main room. She started to back out, and stopped

In the tiny bathroom, the cat was perched on the toilet seat. It scowled at her.

She backed the rest of the way out, crowding Morgan and blocking his view. She would think about that later.

Cargo Trouble

"Change your mind?" Morgan's voice was getting smoother, brighter.

"Already taken. We'll put you here." She kicked the panel by the door across the way and stepped in. No cats, no snakes, no creatures of any kind. She dropped the duffel on the sofa. Morgan lifted the strap from his other bag, and placed it beside the first. He dug around the first bag, and pulled out a brown-wrapped parcel.

"Kitchen?"

"This way." She pointed out the crew showers, the gym, the open room, and the media room. As they neared the open door to her rooms, she saw a row of eight small brown packages lining the wall.

Mice.

She stepped up her pace, and had closed the door by the time Morgan got too close. He bent down to inspect the gruesome display.

"That must be the work of the other stowaway. Dock cat from Rosing Station. Guess it's trying to earn its keep."

He reached to poke at a mouse, and then thought better of it. "Seems like a lot." He was right—no way Minnie was eating eight mice a day. At least Frankie thought not.

She bent for a closer look. The mice didn't just look dead—she now knew what dead mice looked like—they looked aggressively dead. "Why do you think they have that stuff around their whiskers? Goopy ears. But I don't see any giant wounds."

Morgan cast her a glance. "Not my specialty. But I might be able to find out. Got a container?"

They continued to the kitchen. Frankie pulled out the outer bag from her frozen-mouse purchase—not really needed this trip, apparently—and handed it to Morgan. He waved his hand no, thanks.

"No rush. They're already dead. Let's do the fun part first." He presented her with the wrapped package.

Frankie untied the simple string around the plain paper. Inside was a giant bag of peppermint candies. Even the capital cities didn't have such luxury.

"Bought out the kiosk's stash."

She looked at him hard. "That must have been as much as a ticket to Smithson."

He shrugged. His shirt, colors quiet now, whispered with his movement. "I wanted you to be glad you took a risk on me." He leaned against the galley and grinned, more at himself than her. "Your face eating that ice cream. Such bliss."

"You like these, too?"

"I don't know. Never tried." That smile again.

Well. She knew exactly what to do with these. Frankie opened the bag and took two of the thumbnail-sized lozenges out. The rest she put in the freezer. If she wanted another one, she'd have to thaw it out first.

"Then I'll show you the best way to enjoy them." She searched around the cupboard for the special tea. "Thirsty?"

"Indeed."

Tea in pot, hot water in pot. Cups and pot and small dish for the mints, all on a tray. She lifted the tray and turned to head over to her nook. The cat was back, now lounging on the back of the seat in the middle, watching them as if taking measurements.

Frankie set the tray on the table. "Voila. High Tea on the cargo ship Spear."

Morgan, for once, wasn't on her heels. "That's a—" He paused, swallowed. "Cat."

"Stowaway Number One, yes."

"Oh," he looked relieved, who knew why. "It's not yours then." He slid into the seat the cat had taken up this morning as Frankie prepared their tea. Looked like she had a new place in the nook pecking order.

"It belongs to Rosing Station, I guess. I don't even know its name. It wouldn't let me scan it this morning."

Before she'd even finished the sentence, Morgan had leaned toward the cat. Fast as laser light, he grabbed it behind its head, turned it along his forearm, spread away some fur by its neck, and released it. Both the cat and Frankie stopped, startled.

Then the cat started to lick its paw, all casual. Ignoring it, the move seemed to say. Frankie took its lead and slid into her seat.

"Here's what you do," she said. "Put the mint on your tongue. Don't swallow it! You can suck on it a little to get the flavor going. Take a sip of the tea, let it run over the mint, and swallow that." She showed him.

That first sip brought with it so many memories Frankie thought she might faint. Summer at the beach. Solstice holidays. Extra-special birthday treat, this time only—every time. She closed her eyes. That life had been so sweet.

"That's the face," Morgan said.

She didn't open her eyes until the peppermint itself was a memory.

Chapter Eight

The tea pot was cold, the cat was asleep, and Morgan was reading his tablet when Frankie came back to the present. She straightened in her seat, startled.

Both stowaways looked up. The cat went back to sleep. Morgan glanced at his tablet again, turned it off, and set it down. "Welcome back to this sector."

"My mind did go far away this time." she clasped the tea saucer in two hands. "It was nice."

"So," he started. "About the cat."

"I know! Isn't it a monster. I didn't know they came that big. At least the domesticated kind."

"Right." For some reason, Morgan looked uncomfortable. "It's a girl, which is good because they are usually calmer. She's spayed, so no little monster kitties are coming anytime soon. And her name is Spike."

The cat perked up at the sound of her name.

"Seriously? Can you rename cats?"

"Not if they're not yours, you can't." He tilted his head, teasing. "Besides, your ship is called Spear, and it looks like a mecha snowman. I thought you would like it."

At Frankie's blank look, he lifted his hand and started drawing a picture in the air. "Snowman: big circle for his bottom, medium circle his middle, little circle his head." He punctuated the drawing with single-dot eyes and a wide smile. "What I can't figure out is why we're here in the middle and not in the head."

He didn't know much about cargo ships. "Engine and all the exploding parts are in there. That way, if boom, cargo is safe. Safer."

"We're the protective barrier? Great fun." He stretched his long arms and legs. "Guess I'll go get your critters, then. Take them to the stable. There's a mini-lab in there. It's calibrated for horses, but I'm sure we can dial it down."

He took the bag from where Frankie had left it on the galley counter. "Want to come with? You can see a live horse, up close."

Frankie wasn't ready yet to tense up her muscles to move. "I've seen horses."

"But have you seen galaxy-famous racing stallions? I thought not."

"Yes, I have." She shouldn't have said that, but it was true.

"Where ever did you— ?" He held up his hand. "Nope. We agreed. No delving into backgrounds."

She watched him pass, heard the soft groan of disgust amid the apparent shuffling of dead mice into the bag. "She could have eaten a couple," Morgan said.

"Who knows that she didn't? Eight's a lot." She rested her hands on the cushion to each side of her. Orange wasn't so bad. "You know how to manage the airlock, right?"

"Aye, captain." A pause. "You won't lock it on me, will you?" The waver in his voice was back. He wasn't as serene as he pretended.

Cargo Trouble

"Of course not," she was in the middle of saying when the alarm claxon pierced the air.

Frankie jumped to her feet, bashing into the table. Spike at least landed on her paws on the seat cushion after startling herself aloft.

"What is it?" Frankie shouted at her wristcom as she dragged herself out of the nook, even though the room had good sound pickup. She swiped open the pilot screens, two panels of controls and a wide viewscreen, and searched for red across the gauges.

All green.

She widened the viewer to all cameras, and scanned for incoming trouble. She'd never moved so fast.

Nothing.

"Ship!"

"Cargo hold. Crewmember Minnie. Life signs red. Drone activated, sent for visual."

What could a drone do? Would Minnie even let it touch her?

Frankie was running for the stairs before she remembered Morgan was in the hall. He caught her before she barreled into him, spun, and let her go. "I'll follow."

Down the hall, down the stairs, quick, quick.

"Severe convulsions. Acidosis imminent."

Acidosis wouldn't be so bad, Frankie rationalized as she slammed her hand on the inner door panel. She slipped through before it was fully open and slapped the next panel. "Where? Map on my comm. Hold lights on bright!"

A moment of blindness as every light in the hold powered on. Frankie was nearly off the walkway before she remembered to stomp her boots grav-on. The map showed halfway along, but nearer the hull than the walkway. She got to the spot, and looked down.

Minnie's body floated, unanchored. Whipsawing, as if a giant child had hold of her middle and was shaking her back and forth. She was keening.

Frankie already had the closest emergency box open and was tying the line around her waist. She locked the anchor clip on the railing and stomped off her boots.

Minnie's flailing wasn't stopping. She should be way into acidosis by now, minutes after the claxon.

It was not going to be death throes.

Frankie gauged the distance and angle again, kicked herself over the railing and then turned her boots on. She dropped as fast as a blink.

Aim true, she had hands on Minnie, close to head, close to middle. Together, they landed on the hull.

Minnie wasn't stopping. The snake's eyes were glassy, but she was still keening. Not dead yet. Not going to be dead.

"She's hurt?" Ship had linked Morgan into the comms.

"Sick, I think."

"Bring her to the stables. I'll pull your line there."

Minnie must have roused enough to know Frankie was with her. As they lifted and started to swing toward the stables, the snake pulled its tail in, wrapping it around Frankie's middle. "I'm here," Frankie whispered toward Minnie's head, which she still held a bit away from her. The mouth had foam around it. "We've got you."

Morgan moved quickly, too. As he dropped onto the stable box, and then short-hopped to the hull nearest the smaller opening in his container, he was talking to someone. She hoped it wasn't her, since she wasn't hearing it.

He pulled her in hand over hand. At the container, she tried to grav-on as gently as possible.

"Double entry, but portals, not like yours," Morgan said. "You'll have to step up. He spun the wheel that opened the portal and then swung it wide. Minnie's head crossed the threshold first as Frankie stepped over the short barrier. Morgan held Minnie's tail out of the way as he wheeled the door closed one-handed. Then the second, inner door.

Frankie's gaze was on the snake in her arms and the portal she was stepping through as she entered the space, a bright, brilliant white.

"I've turned all the lights on, sir," a cultured voice said. "And closed the door to the stallions. They shouldn't be able to scent on her."

A synthetic person stood beside the largest examination table Frankie had ever seen. They had a cart of medical-looking implements at their side. Aqua-blue antiseptic gloves on their hands. The mirrored light above the table cast a halo around their head.

"Elvin, this is Captain Styles. Captain, this is Doc Elvin, the best veterinarian in the sector."

Elvin cleared their throat. "With horses," they said, but added, "who move just as much on the table as your friend, there."

Frankie didn't take the time to wonder at a fully-stocked veterinary facility hidden in her hold, nor at the fact that there was, indeed, another stowaway. She held Minnie's head sideways to Elvin, who took it gently. Minnie was still spasming, but more gently. Pulsing rather than thrashing. And still, barely, keening.

Frankie spun slowly in place to unwind her friend, keeping her hands on whatever part was nearby. With Elvin and Morgan's help, she got all of Minnie on the table. Good thing it was so big.

"Captain. you take the head, in case—"

"Minnie," Morgan said.

"In case Minnie can see or smell. She knows you best, and that would make her more comfortable."

Frankie went around the table to the edge closest to the horse-door. She put both hands on Minnie, sending all her most comforting thoughts. Please, please, girl, stay with me. Minnie's eyes were open and glazed. The green-white foam wasn't coming out of her mouth anymore. It had crusted along the sides.

Elvin deftly rearranged Minnie so her coils lay flat, if twitching. He pointed to two spots where Morgan should put his hands. After a moment's hesitation, he did as directed.

Elvin took a tool from the cart and waved it steadily along Minnie's length, starting at the mouth. "Big meal," he said. "I see three new mice at the top of the stomach. One part-digested lower down."

"I gave her that one yesterday."

Elvin kept scanning. "No internal injuries past the meal. Nothing wrong at this end." They set the scanner down and ran their hands along Minnie. "No reaction to touch, here where the meal is, or where it isn't."

Her breaths were slowing, now that the spasms weren't pushing air out. "Hurry," Frankie said.

Elvin nodded. "Something to do with the meal. I don't want to take the time to find out exactly what. We need to get it all out first, then clean up what's already in her system after."

Morgan slid a hand up to cover one of Frankie's. "What do we have to do? Reach down her throat?"

"Surgery. Faster and less invasive. We can get the three out through one cut, and the earlier one through another."

Frankie squeezed Minnie softly. "But can she stand that?"

"We need to sedate her, at least a little bit. She's out right now, but I don't want her moving mid-extraction." Elvin pulled an aerosol can out from the cupboard behind them. "I can't give her this—it will tranquilize a horse. But I think a little spray, and wave it in front of her nose, should do it."

They spritzed a bit onto a giant bandage, and handed it to Frankie. "Don't you breathe too much of it in, either."

Cargo Trouble

Frankie took the bandage and waved it in front of Minnie twice. Almost immediately, the spasms eased, and her breathing evened out.

Frankie's breathing was not evening out. She pictured the worst as Elvin laid out his scalpel, antiseptics, bandages, and an exceptionally sharp pair of forceps. She swayed. Elvin grabbed her arm.

"I'm fine," she said. "Just, Minnie."

"In process. Morgan, let's put the ether in a bag for now. Top drawer behind you."

Morgan had a bag in seconds, without taking his other hand from Minnie. He flicked it open and held it out for Frankie to drop the bandage in. Once sealed, he handed it back to her and took his place.

"We're going to start," Elvin said. "Captain, can you tell us a bit about Minnie, here?" They used another bandage to sanitize the surgical site.

Frankie looked up at the vet. "She... she conveyed with the ship. Old Peters and her, they've been together a long time. He left last week, and I think she really misses him."

As the blade neared Minnie's body, Frankie shut her eyes tight. She felt a slight pull, but Minnie didn't seem to react.

Morgan cleared his throat. "How can you tell?"

Frankie had to smile. She looked at him, but he shook his head. "One more minute."

"Right." She kept her gaze on him. "Well, I didn't move into captain's quarters until the second day we were on our own. Wanted to change the sheets, air things out, all that." Peters favored some ancient perfume that would only attract selkies.

"We keep most of the doors open, when nobody else is on-ship," she said. "So Minnie doesn't wake us up all the time going in and out of places. I don't know when she came in that night.

There's a big tree thing she likes to drape on when she sleeps. When I woke up next morning, I was so comfortable, tucked tight, so warm and cozy. And then I remembered, I was on-ship, in a big bed, by myself."

Morgan choked off a laugh.

"You're right. Minnie was in with me. Under the covers! Snoring like the giant snake she is. Lucky I don't startle so easily."

"Done," Elvin said. "Sealing the cuts now, very small. Stomach sealed easily, and we'll figure something out about these scales."

Minnie's eyelids had closed. Frankie bent closer to feel the snake's breath. Still there.

Elvin swept up his tools and set them aside on the cart. "I think it's the mice. It might be hard to tell, because they're mixed in with gastric juices." They looked at Frankie. "But we'll try."

Frankie reached up to wipe her eyes; they were wet somehow. Both Elvin and Morgan grabbed for her hand. Morgan was fastest.

"Might want to wash the tranquilizer off first. And doc, I think I might have something for you." He pulled the bag of dead mice out of a pocket. "Ship's cat gave us these. No stomach juice: She wisely didn't chew on them first."

"Smart cat," the doctor said. As they went to a corner where the lab must be, Frankie crawled onto the table. She lay along Minnie, touching as much of the snake as she could. She closed her eyes. She was so tired.

A moment later, she felt a soft blanket settle over them both. The bright part of the light over the examination table winked off, but the heat part kept buzzing, sending warmth into the blanket.

She woke halfway to feel Minnie draping herself along top of her. She fell back into slumber, smiling.

Cargo Trouble

Frankie opened her eyes to find two people sitting in straight-backed chairs, watching her. The human one spoke first.

"You spend a lot of your day with your eyes closed," Morgan said.

She pushed herself up and swung her shins down, and she was seated just as they were, except on a metallic table and with a giant snake draped across her shoulders and into her lap.

"You are not a serious person," she said.

"Captain," Elvin said. We think we know what happened. Approximately." They looked at Morgan.

Morgan rubbed his eyes, which looked almost bloodshot. His hair did not look perfect.

"You want the good news, or the bad?" he said.

Chapter Nine

Infestation. Worse, the mice carried some sort of toxin—toxic even to them, apparently.

Elvin raised a screen showing their scientific findings, which only made Frankie's caffeine-deprived brain swim.

Morgan interrupted with words that made sense. "We found the box. The cat led us to it. It was some singleton labeled as coming from Stackfield."

"There was no Stackfield cargo. Is that a coffeemaker over there?"

Elvin rose gracefully and moved to the tiny shelf that must be their entire kitchen in here. They'd dimmed the lights, but the room was still super white and sterile. One room, two-thirds this table she sat on. Two portholes, one over the other, that must be the capsule beds. And a door behind which stomped and snorted two giant mammals. It was easy to see how a person might get cabin fever locked in here, unless they really loved horses.

Plus a synth. She'd think about that news later.

"Single box. Beans?"

She frowned. "Adzuki beans, weird. Last-minute add. Double rate." Never take cargo you don't know anything about, Old Peters had said. And here she was, proving his point, stowaways galore. Some great captain. She hadn't even had the ship scan the cargo. "But the inspector herself vetted it."

"Did she say that?"

She couldn't remember. "I guess I assumed it was safe. Inspectors inspect, right?" The scent of coffee brewing reached her nose. The pain between her eyes eased. "Anyway, so this box," she prompted.

"The box, so it was designed with corners that the mice could gnaw through. Elvin thinks it took most of a day. Then the critters were free to roam the hold."

Elvin handed her a cup of the blessed brew. Frankie breathed it in, washing away a bit of the panic that was building inside her chest. She took a careful sip, but it was the perfect temperature.

"So the grain is ruined," she said. "Infected." And she was on the hook for its whole cost, since she didn't have portering insurance yet.

"Well, there's your good news," Morgan said, accepting his own saucer of brew. "Thanks, Elvin. Whoever set the trap up got their timing wrong. The mice hadn't made it far out of their cage before they started to die."

"Seizures and spasms," Elvin said. "Like this one, here." They stroked Minnie gently, away from her head. The snake sighed in her sleep.

"So—more good news—Minnie didn't eat any live mice. The toxin took longer to get into her system, even though she downed three of them."

Elvin stroked her again. "And she is clear of it. Temperature steady. Her color should improve within a day, and her energy."

Cargo Trouble

"She's always this color," Frankie said, gazing at Minnie's scales. "Faded rainbow white."

"Even better," Elvin said. They patted Frankie's hand softly, and then turned back to their chair.

Morgan looked impatient at the interruption. "It's a rare toxin, actually plant-based, which is another link to Stackfield."

"But the grain?"

"The grain is fine. Elvin and I scanned it not an hour ago. Spike was guarding the closest crate, and batting any mouse that came near. But we didn't see any live ones there."

Frankie shivered. Close call. Too close. She lifted Minnie from around her shoulders and started the uncoiling process. "We need to check and doublecheck. Could I borrow your scanner? And Elvin, do you have another of those zipped-bags? I could use that for cleanup."

Morgan was faster, pulling out bags. "I'll help," he said. "Need to earn my keep, you know."

Frankie laid Minnie's tail across her coils. "Someone needs to stay with her."

Morgan bumped his fist lightly on Elvin's shoulder. "This guy can do it. Turns out, he doesn't have grav-boots."

"True," Elvin nodded solemnly. "I was quite the flight risk until we got me tethered."

Morgan laughed, as if they were going on a picnic instead of cleaning up a murder scene. "I swear, that Spike gave us such an evil eye when we went to scan the other cargo. Not only infringing on her territory, but in the flopsiest upside-down way you could imagine."

Elvin opened a lower drawer and pulled out a fleeced jacket. He handed it to Frankie, who only then realized she was wearing only her work tunic and leggings. And that she needed to remember Elvin was a he.

"Need to keep your body temperature up," he said. "For Minnie."

Mice were everywhere. Most floated near the box they had escaped, but an intrepid few were near the walls of the hull, bumping against other cargo. A few had even made it to the running lights, as if they were a homing beacon.

"Where are we going to put them all?" Frankie said, looking down at the box from the walkway. Tiny brown bodies everywhere. Farther down, she could see Spike, as advertised, tucked by a handhold on the nearest grain container. That cat deserved a raise.

"Put 'em back in the box they came in." Morgan said. "All the ones in there now are dead. We can seal the opening when we're through." He gazed at her, appraising. Did she look as stupefied as she felt?

"Captain. How about you go scan the cargo again? That will put your mind most at ease, won't it?"

Frankie glared. "Patronizing."

He shrugged. "Am I right?" He pushed himself over the railing and toward the box and its many brown-fuzz satellites.

She did not follow him. He was right. Below the walkway it was easy to tell which way the air currents traveled. Mouse corpses hung along an invisible line from the poison box forward, their numbers thinning the farther they traveled. Frankie dropped off the walkway with grav on, plummeting to the hull beside the first box.

Spike watched her fall, and then poked his head over the edge of the top of the cargo. The container was too tall for Frankie to reach the cat, so she just waved inanely. She should eat something soon. Then she took another look at the cat.

Cargo Trouble

It wasn't shivering. How long had it been in here? Most cats had double layers of fur for warmth, but nothing that would stand against spacer chill.

"You want my jacket?" she said, looking up at Spike. She could have sworn the cat snorted. It moved out of sight.

She should eat something soon and sleep soon. She was starting to hallucinate. And she was talking to a cat.

All the cargo scanned clean. After reading the data on the last box, Frankie sagged against its side. She was okay. Everything, everyone, okay.

Water droplets floated out of the corners of her eyes. She stomped her grav on, and curled into a ball sitting on the hull. This could have gone so much worse. Her carelessness had almost killed Minnie! Frankie did not want any death on her conscience. Not in her life. Any more death.

If she wasn't cut out to be a simple cargo pilot, what was she good for? She'd had such advantages, everyone said. Everyone who didn't know better. She wasn't ready to go out on her own, that was what Beth had said. Did she—and even Morgan, a stranger—know Frankie better than she did herself?

Her comm pinged. Morgan. "We're clear over here. Meet me by the inner hatch?"

"Stables. I need to be with Minnie when she wakes up."

"Elvin has her prepped for travel. We used your red floater-thingy. Big warm horse blankets piled on and everything."

He waited for her to answer.

She couldn't.

Poor Minnie.

"Captain," he said, soft. "We need to get Minnie inside. Get her to her own space, comfortable. Tuck her into bed. Right?"

A shadow moved above her. They were passing on the walkway.

Nicky Penttila

Frankie kicked grav off and went to join them.
She left her tears to float.

Chapter Ten

Frankie led Morgan to the near elevator, but she took the stairs. By the time he and Minnie were at her suite entry, she had hit the toilet, grabbed a protein drink in the kitchen, and gotten to the bedroom to throw the covers wide enough for a giant snake. Together, they slid the semi-awake Minnie onto the bed, covering her to her chin. The snake tasted the air with her tongue a couple times, and then slid her head under the covers.

Standing by the bed, Frankie sucked down the drink and did a quick scan of the ship's status screens.

"How often do you do that?" Morgan said. He was inspecting Minnie's tree as if he were going to build one, but he must have heard the screens buzz into view.

"Couple times a day."

He looked at her, as intently as the tree. "You've done it at least eight times in the last hour. That I've seen."

She wiped the screens closed with a little more force than usual. "This is all ... a lot. We need to talk, right? But first I need to get my head straight. I'm tired." At the word, her eyelids started to feel even heavier.

He nodded. He ran his hand along one of the tree's branches. "Sleep would do us both good. And Minnie. All of us. Yeah." He hadn't slept much either. His face was pale from an hour in the cargo hold. And he had been in there earlier, while she was with Minnie, finding the mice. Helping save her hide.

But he'd also hidden things. Lied. And she needed to find out why.

Later. Now she needed his help. Again.

"Morgan?" She skirted around the edge of her bed, slipping to the other side. Keeping her eyes on the lump that was Minnie.

"Anything," he said.

"My doors are set to stay open. Would you leave yours open, too? In case I need to call."

He paused so long she had to look up at him.

"Of course," he said, placing his left hand over his heart.

"Thank you," she sighed out. "It's a long push at the top right of the door panel." Of course he knew that, it was standard. She should stop talking.

She sat—sank—onto the bed. After she set the empty shake bag on her nightstand, she didn't know what to do with her hands. They dropped into her lap.

The gray fog was coming in, thick and deep. She needed to divert the mood, not let it reach her. Not let it devour her like it did sometimes. What was happening now was not as bad as that first time, nothing to drop into the abyss for, she told herself. As usual, her mind listened but her heart kept sinking.

A footstep on the office floor. She couldn't even look up.

"I've got hot miso soup," Morgan said. "For people who take their boots off."

That sounded plausible. Frankie lifted a foot and set it on her

Cargo Trouble

knee. The lacings were icy but familiar, the touch fasteners zipped open fine. The boot fell to the floor. She dropped her hands into her lap, exhausted. Once she'd admitted how tired she was, the cavernous need for panic-processing, event unravelling, history suppression, opened up.

"Boots. Plural."

She must not have moved fast enough. Morgan was kneeling at her foot, lifting it by the heel, slipping the boot off. Handing her a mug of umami steam.

Miso soup had never tasted so good. Even with the borrowed jacket, she'd been chilled frosty. That must be why her thinking was so slow. She should give the jacket back. As soon as she unzipped it and started to pull an arm out, Morgan was there to make it go faster. Somehow he had taken the mug, as well.

Frankie dropped to her side and wriggled under the covers.

Minnie was so warm.

When Frankie awoke, Minnie was draped along the higher branches of her tree, dozing. She allowed Frankie to inspect the two incision wounds, which looked fine.

Frankie rested her forehead on her friend's coils. This could have been so, so worse. Who would send sick mice across space? What were the chances a fully stocked veterinary facility would be in her hold at the same time? And where had she seen that white-cloud logo that was on Morgan's jacket before?

The ship's status screens were clear, and Elvin had sent her a message. She fetched the scanner from the miniwagon, which Morgan had left beside an office wall, and ran it down Minnie's length. She sent the results to the vet. Another message pinged.

"Elvin says you're cleared for food, Minnie-min. I'll go heat up a mouse for you." Frankie shook her head at herself. First she gives Minnie a nickname, now she offers to put a dead rodent into her reheater. Guess we're friends now.

She heard Morgan moving in his room as she passed. He did not come to the kitchen while she warmed the mouse and left it at the base of the tree for Minnie. Giving her space? Hiding?

Whatever, good. Frankie needed to have a private conversation, and it might be better on an empty stomach. Well, except for matcha. She took the small pot with her down the hall to main navigation.

She could pilot the ship from anywhere using her screens, and most of the time it was in long transit it was on autopilot anyway. But sometimes you wanted to touch the panels and turn the keys. And sometimes you wanted a place that wasn't so personal.

Frankie programmed in the ship-to-satellite call, grimacing at the estimate of credits needed. It was worth it, to know. She had to check the local time before trying to figure out what time it was in Stackfield. Almost midnight! Everything off-kilter.

A pause, and the call connected. The first link—ship to satellite—would transmit faster than light. The second—satellite to ground—would be slightly delayed. Memories of trying to reverse-engineer how exactly the system worked threatened to bubble up, but Frankie stamped them down. She needed to focus.

"Frankie? What's wrong?" She didn't see Peters, but his tone was clear. "You know how expensive this is? This call will cost profit off an entire run."

He should stop talking, then. "Listen. How could you load a package of infected mice on my ship?'

"Mice? Is that what you said? I didn't order anything."

Now Frankie wished she'd paid for visual. That would have put

Cargo Trouble

her back a whole circuit's profit. "Addressed to you, your new address, in Stackfield. Labeled adzuki beans. Your favorite."

"Shit."

"Why, Peters?" She couldn't keep the hurt out of her voice.

"No! Frankie, no. Believe me. I would never do that to you."

"Minnie almost died." Now her voice did break. "Doing her job. She ate the poisoned mice." She sniffed back a sob. "We had to cut her open to get them out."

Silence. Then, "My lord. My blooming lord. I know who did it."

"Who, then?"

"Where are you?"

What did that matter? "Halfway to Smithson Station. Ship hit deceleration eight hours ago." They'd been sitting in the kitchen then. So much had happened, in the space of eight hours.

"Two days out, then. Running fast? No, don't answer. That's good." Peters was talking fast, which meant he was thinking fast, which could be good or bad. "You'll be too early for the next pickup. Free a couple of days. Could you meet me at Stackfield Orbital? It will take me as long just to get out there."

She didn't want to see him, even if he didn't try to destroy her cargo and kill her friend. "Can't you just message me?"

"Wouldn't be prudent. Better to meet up. And Frankie?" His voice choked off. He cleared his throat. "I changed my mind. Begging pardon. I want Minnie here. With me."

She was such a fool. Of course, Peters would never harm Minnie. If he'd wanted to sabotage her business, he never—never —would have done it in a way that even hinted at putting Minnie in danger.

"Minnie is fine, now," Frankie said. "She's on her tree—no, she's in the greenroom, basking."

"I will bring her with me when I see you."

Chapter Eleven

As she reconstituted something that called itself NoodleBowlYum, Frankie caught herself checking ship's scanners again. How many times today, already? She had no idea.

She was halfway through the noodles, which had, surprisingly, lived up to their promise, when Morgan entered the kitchen. He, too, looked rested, if a little less put-together than usual. He was wearing the same tunic, still blessedly quiet, but had changed to thicker trousers and crew boots.

Spike followed at his heels. The cat was another puzzle. Why did she stow away? Surely she knew how ships at docks worked. And how had she known not to eat the poison mice?

Morgan opened the breakfast cupboard and inspected its contents. "Okay if I have some of this?" He pulled a packet out and read the label. "Porridge." He moved easily in the confined area, for such a lanky person. He should eat more.

"Have two," she said. "Tea's to the left, coffee's below. There's even some reconstituted juice in the cooler below you. Fruit, but I can't remember which. It's green, but tastes good. There's an open protein chow that Spike likes."

He fed the cat, and then brought her a glass of juice along with his own. Its sharp citrus bite made up for its lack of smell.

She let him eat in peace. She needed to recover from her first hard conversation. What did Peters mean, he knew who did it? Did he have some enemy from the past, shipping toxins without looking to see if Peters was still the pilot? No, the label and manifest both had his new address. She should have noticed that at loading. Should, should, should.

Morgan ate neatly. Capital City manners. She wondered if he'd noticed that about her, too. Deliberately, she lifted her saucer with her wrong hand and drank the dregs of her tea.

He'd already finished his. He lifted his saucer to her—want more? He poured for them both.

"So," he said. "Ask your questions."

Frankie held her saucer in both hands. Its warmth traveled all the way to her wrists.

"First, I want to thank you, and Elvin. Your quick actions and your amazing veterinary lab saved my shipmate's life. We owe you a great debt."

He opened his mouth to speak, but before he could start in, she held up a hand. "And I'm grateful, as well, for your help solving the mouse problem. Without you, and yes, you too, Spike"—the cat was rubbing itself against her shins—"my cargo would have been ruined. People would have gone hungry."

The cat jumped onto the cushion next to Frankie, settled in, and looked at her expectantly. Frankie stroked her head and the soft tufts of her ears. "Thank you, Spike." She leaned back up, and Spike started cleaning her whiskers. She looked at Morgan.

"But," he said.

"But. How did you know to bring a veterinary facility onto the ship? Why this ship? How did you know what was wrong so fast. Wait, there's more."

"No," he interrupted. "I can answer those right away. I did not know anything about anything to do with your shipping. I swear to you. I got kicked off my transport and I knew you were young and hungry."

"How did you know anything about me?"

"I didn't! No, seriously. Everyone can tell. Your captain's tag is still shiny. You need to dull it a little if you want to be taken for an old-timer."

Frankie glanced down at the tag. He was right.

"I did not bring poison onto your ship," he said.

Right. "But you brought an undeclared micro-gravity device. Otherwise, the stable would have no gravity." Micro-grav units, some as small as a miniwagon, were extremely rare—and extremely prone to overheating and exploding. Frankie had never dreamed she'd encounter one.

"It's freezing in the hold. Nothing's going to overheat." Morgan stopped. Frankie waited him out in silence. It took a full minute.

"You're right. I should have told you. But I needed to get to Smithson. I had to! This deal is the end of my career in horse-trading. I need it to stay in the black. I absolutely need it." He turned his palms up, shrugging. "I regret the error."

She'd come back to that. "In addition, you contrived to bring onboard a person who is considered illegal in Cooperative space."

"Elvin's not illegal. He has papers showing he's part of an experimental cohort."

Frankie crossed her arms. "Of veterinarians?"

"No, of course not." He ran his fingers through his hair, both sides at once. It reminded Frankie of a swimmer pulling out of the water and onto the side of the pool, pushing the water from their face. But his face didn't look so serene.

"Yes, he shouldn't be out here. He's supposed to stay at home, on the compound. But he's still legal! Only, it's better if no one knows about him."

Frankie shook her head. "Then why is he even out here?"

"He's a great vet! I need him to, um." He paused. "Keep the horses healthy. Perfect."

"You're doping the horses!" She slammed her hands on the table. Morgan jumped. Spike opened an eye and closed it again. Frankie didn't know much about horse races, but she did know that many kinds of enhancement were forbidden in contests of that kind. "You're using Elvin's skills, and his precarious situation, to force him to do something illegal for you."

Morgan looked sheepish. "Kind of. But not really! It's not illegal, just a little to the side of the rules. You know, if you read them strictly."

"Elvin does it, and you have deniability. Your hands stay clean." Frankie didn't know why the idea made her so bitter.

"It's not like that." He was a bad wheedler. "Well, it is, but not exactly. I can explain."

She shut that off with a wave of her hand. "I won't tell anyone about your 'friend.' But I want that exploding grav-box out of my hold first we get to Smithson. And you, too."

"And you," she leaned over to stroke Spike again. "You get one more run, then off."

There were way too many beings on this ship. She couldn't wait to be alone.

Chapter Twelve

One could have described the next two days aboard the Spear as calm if one ignored the undercurrents of regret and distrust that wafted throughout the ship.

Elvin had politely declined Frankie's offer to bunk in the main segment. He said it was because he preferred to keep a close eye on the horses. If there even were any horses. He probably didn't want to be around Morgan, who held the synth's safety in his careless, thoughtless, hands.

Frankie scanned the cargo three times a day, to be absolutely sure. She could not seem to stop herself from continually checking the system-scan screens. She'd deal with that compulsion after the trip.

Once, she found Minnie coiled up next to the floor panel for the outer portal to the cargo hold. The snake quivered. Frankie knelt and set her palms on her friend.

"Don't want to go in there? I don't blame you a bit." She stroked the white-of-all-colors length, so solid, so warm. She hadn't eaten the first mouse Frankie had left, rolling it underneath the miniwagon. But the second one, this morning, had disappeared.

"You're off the job, Minnie. I'm taking you to live with Old Peters. You'd like that, wouldn't you?" Frankie tugged Minnie gently to uncoil. "Up, up."

Minnie unraveled from the floor and raveled up Frankie's torso and arms. Thus precariously balanced, Frankie pushed to stand. She walked her friend to the greenroom. The humidity hit them both like a tonic.

Minnie dropped into her nest and settled in. Frankie looked at the nest enviously.

Where was her own safe nest?

Frankie was initialing the manifest for the assistant dockmaster when Morgan walked off the ship through the dock entry, together with his cargo. The cargo traveled on, but he stopped beside her and waited for her to be free.

After she acknowledged him, he bowed prettily. "Thank you for your hospitality—and generosity. I know I was not the most well-behaved guest." He gestured toward the cargo, now being diverted to a side pier. "Would you like to observe the inspection? Make sure you get paid, and all."

After all that had happened, Frankie was still curious about the horses. What were they like? How could they possibly put up with space travel? In her limited experience of them, horses didn't like anything out of the ordinary. Space travel was out of the ordinary to the Nth degree. She nodded, yes.

"One more question," she said as they walked side by side. Morgan had to hitch his stride so she could keep up. "That jacket I borrowed. It had a familiar logo, but I couldn't place it. Is it where you work?"

He winced. "Hoped you hadn't seen that. I used to work there, a while back. Not now. That company is long gone and best forgotten. I'm surprised you recognized it."

"I didn't, exactly. What was the name of it, again?"

Morgan was waving at a person even taller than he was, and in finer clothes. "My buyer. Excuse me a moment."

Frankie stopped, frozen for a moment. Her face went blank. A Skoll. Not one of the two who had harassed her on Rosings, but a more important one.

Morgan hadn't told her a Skoll was the buyer. She didn't care for that omission.

The Skoll saw her, and smiled. "Captain!" they said, closing the gap between them. "Pleasure to meet you. Such an improvement over that bent-back Old Peters."

A rude Skoll. Shocking. Frankie did not smile.

Morgan stepped up. "Frankie, this is Skoll Shara. I take it, Shara, you already know of Captain Styles."

"The captain has something that belongs to us." The Skoll's smile twisted. "We hope she finds herself ready to return it now, after—shall we say—such a difficult trip."

Frankie struggled to keep her composure. The Skolls. Steer clear, Old Peters had said, and she'd tried. They hadn't steered clear of her.

They could have easily bribed the dockmaster on Rosings—they owned half the station. They knew Peters was gone and could easily have found his new address. They knew the Spear was carrying grain.

They couldn't have known about Minnie.

The Skoll took her nonresponse as a cue to keep talking. "And your stalwart companion? Snakes make such good mousers, don't you agree?"

They knew.

Frankie saw red.

Morgan stepped directly between the two, holding a hand up at each of them. She glared at him. Didn't he see what they had done?

"Great to meet, everyone. And here's the examiner now. How about we go and get this done, and the captain can watch with the rest of the crowd?"

Frankie noticed the crowd for the first time. A good hundred people, seated to the side of what must be a viewing area. Drone cameras and two live reporters had the spots directly in front. Only the up-high rows of seats were still empty. She took the back stairs to get to them, avoiding Skoll Shara, who seated themself in the first row.

So these were horse people. They looked like regular people, with really nice boots. Maybe a little overintense in their expression. Their gazes were all rigidly fixed on the two horses stepping nervously out of Morgan's container.

And rightly so. Frankie had never seen such beautiful horses. Browner at the head shading to black at the other end, they were a matched pair. Morgan, tall as he was, barely came up to their withers. Coats so shiny! Elvin must have done something there.

At the thought of the synth, Frankie pulled her gaze away from the action and toward the container. The doors were already shut. Morgan had led the pair out, and stood alone with them as they were scanned, prodded, and, apparently, found acceptable. The inspector nodded and noted something on their tablet. They shook Morgan's hand.

Skoll Shara rose and joined them. Another handshake. Morgan handed the horses' reins to the Skoll, a process that took longer than it should because they had to wait for the photographers to get the shot. The Skoll quickly transferred the reins to a small person, probably a jockey, who led them toward a type of entry Frankie hadn't seen before, for animals.

Morgan was watching the trio intently. As they passed through the opening, which was thick like it had a scanner embedded, his shoulders eased. He looked at his wristcom and nodded.

Show over for now, the people in the stands dispersed quickly. It wasn't all that warm on the docks. Frankie stayed where she was, browsing through all the horse-related products and services advertised in the local feed. She heard someone coming up the back stairs.

Morgan sat on the same bench Frankie sat on, a couple people's width away. He didn't look at her. He made a show of wiping something from his wristcom toward her. She felt the ping, and saw the payment notification.

Still not looking at her, Morgan leaned his elbows on the bench above them. "I've a bit of a problem," he started, and stopped.

Frankie looked away. So many beautiful personal craft in the near docks. The Spear had already been ordered to vacate their inner slip before the next shift, in a few hours. "Not my problem," she said.

"I understand. I do. But I fear for my friend. Our friend."

Frankie leaned back herself. She blew out a long breath. "Fine. I'll take the container, and all it contains, back to Rosings. Standard fee."

"No hazard surcharge?"

How dare he sound amused. "I studied up on that, ah, propulsion system of yours. As you say, overheating is the only risk. Not fair to charge you."

"Not fair," he said slowly. He sat up to use his wristcom. Another payment pinged to Frankie.

She stood, facing away from him. "I'll get it loaded right away. The Spear can't stay in inner dock, so I'm taking her to Stackfield system to wait until my cargo—my other cargo—is ready."

She heard Morgan stand, turn away, turn back toward her. "Captain. Frankie." Even as her brows rose at the familiarity, she turned without thinking.

"Thank you," he said. "I mean it. It was so ... nice to take a trip as just a person, not an Infamous Name. Yes, even though half of it was in a terrifying capsule cabin." He held his hand out to her.

She had to take it. They were in business together.

"Nice while it lasted," he said.

"It was nice to meet you, too," she said, on automatic. Then amended, "Well, interesting."

His laugh was warm as ever. "Safe travels."

"Clear skies," she said.

Chapter Thirteen

Stackfield Orbital Station hadn't changed in the two weeks since Frankie had set Old Peters down on it. A tiny hub with giant docks attached and spinning, a geostationary albino spider. It was best to come in directly from above, if you were a spacer; below, if you were a groundling.

Frankie had already sent in all the many documents to allow formal entry to the planet for a pale giant snake. Minnie's head-only eyes-front-and-open photo was only a little blurry. Once again, Elvin and his lab were a blessing: He could perform all thirteen required tests and supply the results in the proper formats. Minnie was already conditionally approved for immigration by the time the Spear had moored. No quarantine needed.

The adjutant dock chief met them at their berth, peered briefly into Minnie's industrial strength carry crate, and signed off. He looked more askance at the tree.

"It's art," Frankie said. She and the very helpful little bot had managed to get it down into the hold and levered it rather precariously onto the red miniwagon. Minnie's crate had its own slight propulsion, little puff-jet boosters that kept her comfortable when the ship did slingshot maneuvers and the like.

Frankie signaled the hatch to close and lock. She hoped that this wasn't a place that scanned ships without permission. Most stations this far out were live-and-let-live. Closer to Central, you couldn't be sure. Elvin couldn't hide, exactly, he said, but he could stay very still and turn his temperature down.

"I do have the proper papers, remember," he'd said in the lab as he was busy convincing Minnie he did not have a needle and was not about to draw blood.

"Yes, but. Papers." She'd searched for words. "What if they don't ask before they shoot?" Synthetic humans like Elvin were banned, on point of death. For the first time, she wished Morgan was here. To talk her down. To talk dock security down. Just to talk.

"I understand." Elvin said, blood competently obtained. He turned away from her to set the needle in the test kit. "You would not be blamed if I were apprehended, in any case."

"Who cares about that!" Maybe she should, but he'd saved Minnie and therefore was the Hero of the Spear. "I worry about everyone on my ship." She squeezed Minnie so hard she squeaked in protest.

Elvin turned back. He set a rubber-gloved hand over Frankie's. "I am worried, too. But this is not the first trip like this I've taken. How does Morgan put it? Ah. The odds of success are stacked in our favor. It would be dumb not to play."

Yet again, he had politely declined her offer to bunk in the warmth and space of the center segment; this time he gave no reason. So she left him there, in his shining bright caravan in the cargo hold.

Cargo Trouble

Frankie was barely past the gate into the station proper when she saw Old Peters. He didn't look so old now. Already his spacer pallor was less. He had a new chair that looked like it had little boosters as well as wheels.

He looked guilty.

He spoke first. "Frankie! And my so, so pretty Minnie, too," he cooed at the crate. Minnie launched herself at the latched opening. "Give us a minute to get away from the scaredy-cats. I know a place." He looked past the crate. "And the reptile stand, too?"

He did not look her in the face. His gaze darted everywhere else.

"I thought she should have it. I sure won't be using it." Frankie looked at it again from his point of view. "Might need to ship it separately."

"Maybe not. We'll call it art." He pivoted and rolled to the left. "Arboretum's this way. Best spot on the station."

Nearly every station had a greenroom, but few had devoted a full one-third of its area to plant life as had Stackfield Orbital. The station's profit came from selling healthy cuttings and seedlings to ships for their own greenrooms.

The arc of the hull here was made of some almost transparent material. The local sun shone down, bathing the trees and bushes. Deeper in, the flora grew shorter, grasses and flowers. In the center sat a pond big enough for small people to float in foot-powered boats shaped like swans. Peters took them slightly away from the families and toward a clearing of grasses between tall trees. He'd been here before—he beelined straight for an almost-hidden bench in dappled shade.

Frankie hadn't left the dock when she'd dropped Peters off. "I can't believe you didn't tell me about this. I would have hopped off for a minute."

"You couldn't slow down. I never saw a baby captain so eager to get to a grain depository." Peters pushed out of his chair and bent to Minnie's crate.

The latch clicked open, and Minnie flowed across Peters' arm, over his shoulders, around his chest, and back again. Her happy-scarf move.

Peters staggered at the force, but caught his balance, chuckling. He let Frankie take his arm and help him get settled on the bench. Minnie's head swiveled back and forth, tasting the mesmerizing mixture of scents. She even tasted Frankie's hair when she didn't get out of the way fast enough.

Frankie powered down the crate and the wagon, and then sat next to Peters. The clearing was almost empty of people; just a few nappers on a blanket in the sun. Moist air kissed her face. She breathed it in deep. The place was calming her.

She wasn't sure she wanted to be calm.

Peters wasn't going to talk, so Frankie started. "Tell me."

"I'm so sorry, Frankie. I didn't think this would happen. Never in a billion years."

She stretched her arms out, so the sun's light touched the back of her hands.

"The Skoll," he started, and stopped.

She waited, a slow count of thirty. "The Skoll," she said, looking up at a tree that appeared to be a perfect triangle. "Steer clear, you said."

"Already too late for that, I guess."

She dropped her gaze to Peters. He was trying to look at her, almost succeeding. "Did you really agree to sell out to them?" she said.

"No!" His gaze briefly met hers. "But the way they talk, of understandings, of agreements. I said I wasn't interested. I stayed under the radar."

Cargo Trouble

She set her hands on her thighs and stretched out booted feet out to the light. "Why do they even care?"

"They don't. I don't think they do. Thing is, they're collectors. They want everything. There were two of us, holdouts. We thought they'd forget. The routes aren't that big."

Minnie flowed down Peters's legs and out into the sun-warmed grass in front of them. She kept hold of his ankle, though. Peters sighed.

"The other one, Smalls, she sold out a little bit ago. The pressure on me went up. But you were here, better than the Skoll. They don't even like snakes."

"And you didn't tell me this—why?"

He faced her directly. "I talked to them, I did. Explained the situation. You were no threat; you weren't going to poach any Skoll cargo. They didn't need to worry."

They weren't worried. Frankie slid off the bench to sit beside Minnie. The smells were stronger here: grass, loam, wet dog. A hint of lavender or rose? Minnie must be in heaven, after all the years of dulled scents off-planet.

She looked back at Peters. Old Peters, kindly, solicitous, too trusting. "Why didn't you sell?"

His face went fierce. "Why should I? Why should they have such a monopoly? We're the Cooperative, right? We work to the benefit of all, or however that goes."

To one, to all. Frankie had heard the motto all her life. Nearly every day as a child, despite not living on a fully invested Cooperative planet. When she did move, all the way to Central Planets, she heard and saw it constantly.

It had never been true.

"You need to sell, Frankie." Peters sounded defeated. "They'll kill you, and make it look like it was your fault. Just like this time."

Frankie threw herself back on the grass. She had to cover her eyes with a forearm; already the sun had burned red spots in her vision.

"No," she said.

"You can't win. Now that I see how this played out, I can see that they've done this kind of thing before. They said Smalls had a heart attack and needed to retire. Suddenly, she had a nice place on-base, after her pacemaker surgery. There were other times, too."

"I don't want to. Like you said, they shouldn't win." She was sick of venal people succeeding while good people suffered. When would it end?

"They only want the contract. They'll give up the Spear. You could find something else. You're so clever. You can make it work anywhere."

Move systems? Galaxies? With what bankroll? She was in the black, thanks to Morgan, but only just. And nothing in savings. She could beg from Beth; her friend had her own settlement nest egg.

But once she admitted to Beth that she couldn't make it on her own, that would be it. Any help from that end would come with strings attached. Not just strings, but thick cables. Beth would insist that Frankie stay in Central system. Where Frankie absolutely did not wish to be.

Minnie must have sensed Frankie's shifting mood. A heavy coil thumped onto her belly like a friendly punch. "You too? Fine. I'll think about it."

Peters let out a breath. "Best I could hope for."

Later, Frankie walked with them to the departure lounge. Peters had to buy an extra one-way ticket for the tree, which, while art, also took up a person's worth of room on the shuttle and so counted as a person. Peters said his friend would pick him up at the landing with their own miniwagon.

"Creek still wasn't too sure about bunking with Minnie," he

Cargo Trouble

said. "But once I told him about the stand—I called it a tree, like you do—he's all onboard. Says it will be our conversation piece."

Frankie took the long way back to the ship so she could walk through the whole of the garden. She was tempted to swipe a couple blades of grass, but she let the lawn be.

Chapter Fourteen

Frankie couldn't sleep. As the Spear piloted itself back to Smithson Station, she prowled the halls on main deck and upper and lower decks, too. She watched the bots clean the stairwell. She checked all the filters. She just kept moving.

She decided that the cat was avoiding her. She'd heard the door slide, and glimpsed Spike's tail heading toward "her" toilet. But that was all she'd seen of her the rest of the day and night. The half a gravy-boat dinner Frankie had left out was gone, though.

Once, she tried the cargo space. She left the walkway retracted, so it would be even more like flying in space. She kicked off near the entry door and flew, flew, flew to the far end of the hull. She stopped, feet first, on the hull, and then flew back.

Something was missing.

Frankie thought about inviting Elvin up for a game of—what? Synths were supposedly super geniuses. Besides, he'd been pretty clear about liking to be alone.

She liked to be alone, too. Or so she'd thought.

Doing the rounds inspecting all the escape pods, most of which looked surprisingly similar to Morgan's jockey-sized sleeping capsules, a thought struck her. She'd never really been alone—absolutely by herself. Never, since she came to Cooperative Space. She couldn't remember much before then.

Even when she thought she was finally on her own, she'd had Minnie. And then the circus of stowaways. But now, finally, she had what she'd thought she always wanted.

The capsule in the pilot's station blinked green for good. Frankie opened the seal to check inside anyway. It opened along its length, like a coffin. She stared at it for a while, and then crawled in. Surprisingly plush, but it could use a pillow. Maybe a blanket.

She pulled the lid halfway down, telling herself it was a test to see how claustrophobic she was. She curled up, wrapping her arm around her knees.

She wasn't sure how long she'd been there when Spike jumped into the capsule. The cat lay where her legs should be, with its shoulder propped up on her butt. She started to purr. Soon they were both asleep and dreamless.

Waiting for a peppermint to thaw so she could have some tea, Frankie read through the Skoll shipping contract once again. The offer was still in the trades and offers database; the family had not retracted the one they'd sent earlier. Not even to lower the price. Clearly an oversight Frankie felt easy about taking advantage of.

The terms and clauses for the trade looked the same as those in the contract she had signed with Old Peters. This one was only for the portering contract, like they'd said. Nothing about the Spear itself.

She could sign it remotely, the database office person's message said. They'd just seen her in the office a month ago, so felt confident she still was who she said she was.

They must also be in the Skoll family's pocket.

Frankie took a deep breath, signed the contract, and sent it. She checked the ship's sensor screens again, and then shut down all screens. She put the peppermint in her mouth and took the teapot and saucer to the greenroom. Minnie's nest turned out to be too disgusting to lounge on, so Frankie sat with her back to the wall, next to the baby-tomato vines. It was misting time for the tomatoes; she didn't mind being misted too. She savored the tea through her mint, and celebrated her return to solvency.

She'd pick up the Smithson cargo, and finish the route at Rosing Station. Drop Spike off there, and then... see.

The tea was gone, the peppermint melted into memory, when the comm pinged. Probably notice that the contract had been co-signed. Frankie turned her screens back on. Not just the contract, but notice that the Smithson shipment was cancelled.

No reason to go there, then. That much closer to the end of her glorious—meteoric, really—career as an outer rings cargo hauler.

She should change their heading to Rosing Station. Take Elvin home, all the way, not just to the station. What else did she have to do?

Have another peppermint.

She was at the kitchen counter staring at a single peppermint, trying to decide if she really needed to wait for it to thaw, when the satellite-to-ship call came.

Chapter Fifteen

Wherever Morgan was, it was loud.

"Sorry!" he shouted. "Wait." The other sounds cut off abruptly. "Now I'm in the toilet. Connection still good?"

"Hello?"

"Listen, Frankie. Where are you? Want to come down to Smithson Prime? The race is tonight, and the place is already rollicking."

"Where are you? Why?" Frankie checked her charts. ETA Smithson thirty-five minutes. She'd moped the whole trip away.

"I'm in the Skolls' box seats here at the track."

"No. Absolutely not." Frankie said.

"Wait, listen! You are golden with the Skolls now. I talked with them, and they understand."

"Understand what? That I sold them the portering contract?"

"You did?" The surprise in his voice made Frankie wince. Some tough pilot she was. "Okay, never mind," he said. "We can sit in the regular stands, no problem. But you do want to see my horses race, don't you?"

She kind of did, she had to admit. See the culmination of this crazy idea of shipping horses around the universe. But it would mess with her schedule.

What schedule? For a moment, she'd forgotten that all her calendar days were now big empty boxes. A trip down planet would delay her inevitable return to the Inner Worlds.

Still.

"I don't have passage. And I can't afford it anyway."

"You just got paid! Hold on." The connection blasted noise again for almost a whole minute. Frankie used the calculator on her screen to determine how much this pause was costing Morgan. Almost the same as a shuttle ride.

The noise cut off. "I'm back. Skolls have an atmo-hopper at Smithson you can borrow. I said you were a pro pilot. You do know how to fly it, right?"

Frankie rolled her eyes. Atmo-hoppers were what everybody trained on. Except Morgan, apparently. "I'm coming into the station now. Where is the hopper berthed." Silence. "What are the berth coordinates?"

Morgan understood that, and gave the coordinates. "Go to the landing nearest the track, Smithson Number Eight. When can you be here?"

"What's the rush? You said I had a few hours."

"Ours is the last race, the marquee event. You'll want to see the earlier ones so you can compare."

Was she really a person who just ran off and went to the races? She was now.

Cargo Trouble

The hopper was where Morgan had said it was. It was bigger—rated for twenty people, not six—but it flew like all the others Frankie had ever piloted.

Smithson Eight looked like a child's dream flycraft play set. Hoppers and standard planes of all shapes and sizes were parked along the tarmac and covering the dirt packed fields around the two landing zones. She pitied the poor person who had to keep track of whose was where.

She slowed and touched down softly. Easy. She powered down and waited for the tower to tell her where to park. She couldn't see the truck that would tow her. She could hop there, sure, but with this much flyware parked in, she expected nobody was being allowed to do that.

The hull door popped open, and Morgan fell in. She could smell the new burn on his palm from the superheated handle.

"Power up! I got the door." He scrambled to his knees and grabbed the inner handle with his unburned hand.

"What's the berth?"

"No! Take off! I need to get off this planet. Sooner is better, Frankie."

She powered back up. The craft was still warm, but the process would still take a few minutes. Then she stopped, and turned. "I thought we were going to the races?"

"Tell you later." He raced down the aisle of the main cabin and thew himself into the copilot's seat. He started strapping in.

"Tell me now."

His hair hung lank. The only color on his face was a mild burn from sun across his cheekbones and the hairline above his forehead. He stared out the side window toward the terminal.

"I don't see anybody," Frankie said. She flicked a lever, changing her scans. "No humanform readings nearby."

"Everybody's at the races. They left a bot in charge here, can you believe it?" His breathing had not slowed. Frankie thought she could see his pulse in the shadow movement of the skin at his temple. Now he watched the engine readings, tracing their rise into the green. He grabbed the copilot's headset. At speed, they were really going to need the noise protection.

"Go, go, go!"

Frankie set her ship's beacon to warn of liftoff. She scanned the skies with her instruments and her eyes. She reversed her course on the navigation screen and checked that it would work. Not three seconds had passed.

"Quick like a bunny!"

All clear. Frankie pushed the throttle, and the hopper actually leaped off the ground. She pushed the engines hard, to cool off the hull as much as she could as well as reach breakthrough velocity. The force pushed them both deep into the chairs.

Morgan still managed to run his hands through his hair, headset and all.

When they broke atmosphere, and all the noise had eased off, Frankie turned to him.

"Now."

He set the headset back in its cradle. "I told them I was expecting you in three hours, an hour before race time. So, we have"—he checked his wristcom—"two and a half hours to get out of this sector."

Chapter

Wherever Morgan was, it was loud.

"Sorry!" he shouted. "Wait." The other sounds cut off abruptly. "Now I'm in the toilet. Connection still good?"

"Hello?"

"Listen, Frankie. Where are you? Want to come down to

Cargo Trouble

Smithson Prime? The race is tonight, and the place is already rollicking."

"Where are you? Why?" Frankie checked her charts. ETA Smithson thirty-five minutes. She'd moped the whole trip away.

"I'm in the Skolls' box seats here at the track."

"No. Absolutely not." Frankie said.

"Wait, listen! You are golden with the Skolls now. I talked with them, and they understand."

"Understand what? That I sold them the portering contract?"

"You did?" The surprise in his voice made Frankie wince. Some tough pilot she was. "Okay, never mind," he said. "We can sit in the regular stands, no problem. But you do want to see my horses race, don't you?"

She kind of did, she had to admit. See the culmination of this crazy idea of shipping horses around the universe. But it would mess with her schedule.

What schedule? For a moment, she'd forgotten that all her calendar days were now big empty boxes. A trip down planet would delay her inevitable return to the Inner Worlds.

Still.

"I don't have passage. And I can't afford it anyway."

"You just got paid! Hold on." The connection blasted noise again for almost a whole minute. Frankie used the calculator on her screen to determine how much this pause was costing Morgan. Almost the same as a shuttle ride.

The noise cut off. "I'm back. Skolls have an atmo-hopper at Smithson you can borrow. I said you were a pro pilot. You do know how to fly it, right?"

Frankie rolled her eyes. Atmo-hoppers were what everybody trained on. Except Morgan, apparently. "I'm coming into the station now. Where is the hopper berthed." Silence. "What are the berth coordinates?"

Morgan understood that, and gave the coordinates. "Go to the landing nearest the track, Smithson Number Eight. When can you be here?"

"What's the rush? You said I had a few hours."

"Ours is the last race, the marquee event. You'll want to see the earlier ones so you can compare."

Was she really a person who just ran off and went to the races? She was now.

The hopper was where Morgan had said it was. It was bigger—rated for twenty people, not six—but it flew like all the others Frankie had ever piloted.

Smithson Eight looked like a child's dream flycraft play set. Hoppers and standard planes of all shapes and sizes were parked along the tarmac and covering the dirt packed fields around the two landing zones. She pitied the poor person who had to keep track of whose was where.

She slowed and touched down softly. Easy. She powered down and waited for the tower to tell her where to park. She couldn't see the truck that would tow her. She could hop there, sure, but with this much flyware parked in, she expected nobody was being allowed to do that.

The hull door popped open, and Morgan fell in. She could smell the new burn on his palm from the superheated handle.

"Power up! I got the door." He scrambled to his knees and grabbed the inner handle with his unburned hand.

"What's the berth?"

"No! Take off! I need to get off this planet. Sooner is better, Frankie."

Cargo Trouble

She powered back up. The craft was still warm, but the process would still take a few minutes. Then she stopped, and turned. "I thought we were going to the races?"

"Tell you later." He raced down the aisle of the main cabin and thew himself into the copilot's seat. He started strapping in.

"Tell me now."

His hair hung lank. The only color on his face was a mild burn from sun across his cheekbones and the hairline above his forehead. He stared out the side window toward the terminal.

"I don't see anybody," Frankie said. She flicked a lever, changing her scans. "No humanform readings nearby."

"Everybody's at the races. They left a bot in charge here, can you believe it?" His breathing had not slowed. Frankie thought she could see his pulse in the shadow movement of the skin at his temple. Now he watched the engine readings, tracing their rise into the green. He grabbed the copilot's headset. At speed, they were really going to need the noise protection.

"Go, go, go!"

Frankie set her ship's beacon to warn of liftoff. She scanned the skies with her instruments and her eyes. She reversed her course on the navigation screen and checked that it would work. Not three seconds had passed.

"Quick like a bunny!"

All clear. Frankie pushed the throttle, and the hopper actually leaped off the ground. She pushed the engines hard, to cool off the hull as much as she could as well as reach breakthrough velocity. The force pushed them both deep into the chairs.

Morgan still managed to run his hands through his hair, headset and all.

When they broke atmosphere, and all the noise had eased off, Frankie turned to him.

"Now."

He set the headset back in its cradle. "I told them I was expecting you in three hours, an hour before race time. So, we have"—he checked his wristcom—"two and a half hours to get out of this sector."

Chapter Sixteen

"We?" Frankie said. She swiped the Spear's screens into view and started its ready-launch sequence.

"I sort of implied we were together. To get them to let you on the planet." Morgan rubbed his face with his hand. "I sort of implied we were a couple. Lovers. Sorry."

Frankie blinked that information straight into her brain's buffer. She'd think about that later.

"So, the deal is, the horses, their hearts aren't exactly right. One or the other may win this race, but if they do, they might have a heart attack before they get to the winner's circle. Or soon after. More likely they'll start to feel bad, and wash out altogether. When that happens, the Skolls will be unhappy. And we should be gone before that."

"But we're going to Rosings. Where all the Skolls live."

"Yeah, we should probably change that." He pointed out the window toward a gray circle in the distance. "We should take the jump-tunnel."

"Jump? Where?" Not to mention the usual backup at jump

tunnels. She would have needed to put in the request hours ago to get a spot soon.

"Doesn't matter."

"It really does, for a jump-tunnel."

"Dyad System, then. It's close but not Rosings." He watched her call up the tunnel authority and start the permission process. "I forgot that part."

"You are not a shit-together person," Frankie said.

The screen to Smithson station blinked green. "Prepare for dock."

She did not put the hopper back in its proper slot, but parked it at the pier right next to the Spear. There was no chance of hiding their tracks anyway. Frankie jumped and Morgan tumbled out of the hopper and up the pilot's ramp.

"Find the cat," she ordered as she sat down in the pilot's chair. "She needs to be secure by the time we hit the tunnel." She told Ship to send Spike's coordinates to Morgan's comm. "Tell Elvin, too."

Then all her attention was taken up arguing with tunnel authority that no, they did have a transit pass already and how could it have gone missing, and she had important live cargo that had to be moved at fastest possible velocity. The phrase actually was "fastest practical velocity," but nothing about this situation was practical.

Her Art of Persuasion class at university actually paid off: They had a "replacement pass" for only an hour from now. Barely enough time for them to get to the gate itself.

Chapter Seventeen

The Spear was ten minutes from the gate, and third in the queue, when the Skolls caught up to them. The ship closing in on them was shaped like a Galactic Patrol cruiser, but wasn't behaving like one. But it could still override Frankie's too-basic communications locks.

"Spear: Stand down. Await boarding." The blast of sound rebounded through the halls and rang in Frankie's ears. She pushed her earphones down around her neck but kept the microphone close. She punched in the patrol transmit code. "Patrol: Assistance needed. Right at the gate at Smithson station." It was an open-channel call. The Skolls would hear it, too. She kept the Spear aimed straight for the jump-tunnel.

"Spear: Stand down or we will shoot. Show us the engines powering down."

Frankie cut the engines in half, which, since they had been decelerating to gate speed, actually boosted the distance between the cruiser and the Spear. They were going to rocket through the tunnel. If they got there.

The message was a full minute delayed. "Patrol acknowledged. Cruiser fifteen minutes out."

So much for that. "Acknowledged. Thank you." The Galactics would be able to cite the Skolls for impersonating an official patrol, maybe, after they cleaned the wreckage of the Spear out of the travel lane.

The second-to-last ship winked through the gate, and the one before their slot moved into position. Frankie was headed straight at that position, no side-tracking. She hoped the very nice midsize pleasure cruiser knew how to set up a quick jump.

She was programming the jump on one screen while keeping an eye on the fake cruiser on another when Morgan stomped in. "Give me communications," he said, dropping into his seat and strapping in.

"That panel has it already, top right. Where is Spike?"

"Isn't she here? I told her to come up. We were in the kitchen, and then she left." He was searching for main comms for the Skoll cruiser with one hand and holding a bunch of pita chips in the other. "Want some?"

Her hands were full, but somehow she managed to flick on all-call. "Spike the cat: Report to the pilot's galley now. Elvin the doc: Please strap in. You have full ship's-view access."

"You know the cat doesn't speak Galactic, right?" Morgan didn't wait for an answer. He cleared his throat and opened a channel.

"Patrol cruiser, this is the cargo ship Bubbles. Why are you chasing us?"

"Don't bullshit us, Spear."

"Seriously?" Morgan actually made his voice squeak. "Who would ever mistake my little snowman for something that deserved such a pointy name."

"What are you doing?" Frankie spared a half-second to glare at

Cargo Trouble

Morgan. He waved his hands, and then signed "playing for time" in passable GSL.

"Stand by," the fake cruiser said.

Seriously?

"Toldja," Morgan said.

"We are powering weapons," the fake cruiser said. "Last chance."

The jump coordinates were set and double-checked. Frankie waved that screen to the side and pulled up a list of possible evasive maneuvers. Not a lot to choose from for a bulky cargo ship in a traffic lane barreling toward a jump-gate.

"Um. Frankie?"

"Spit it out." There was some kind of barrel roll she might be able to finagle, so long as the next ship in the tunnel queue didn't move. At all.

"What kind of shielding do we have?"

"Asteroid evasion. Steep-angle deflection."

"So, none, really. In that case, we should turn around."

"What?" Frankie pulled her fingers away from the screens so she wouldn't flinch and push a panel by mistake.

"Not surrender. But it would be really good if the stable's grav-coil didn't get hit. By anything." They were traveling engine first, as usual, which meant the cargo bay was closest to the fake cruiser's weapons.

Frankie pulled up another screen and started calculating. "If we do a tip-to-toe, we would take damage. And then we'd have our engines in their line of fire. Also bad. Which would be worse?"

Morgan held his hands out. "For us, it's the same. For the tunnel, a direct hit on the grav-box would knock it out of service. Maybe for good."

The last ship before them winked into the tunnel.

Frankie's fingers flew over the panels and controls. "I can do this," she muttered.

Spike jumped onto the pilot's board. Morgan grabbed for the cat. She slipped out of his reach, but away from the control panels Frankie was frantically manipulating. "We're doing this," she warned both of them.

"Target locked. Last chance, Spear."

She didn't have enough fingers.

"Morgan, listen! I need you to press this panel, the moment I say so." She pointed with her pinkie finger toward a panel too far for it to reach. "Pitch thrusters, there. It's all set up."

"Which panel?"

"This one. On my count. Three..."

The first blast went wide. Time seemed to stretch. She saw the moment Morgan froze. Only his gaze followed the powder from the blast reflecting the light as it streaked by.

"Locking target."

"Morgan!"

Spike jumped over to him and bit him on the chin. He shuddered, and came back to life.

"This panel."

"Okay, " he said, reaching over.

Everything under her hands was ready. "Now!"

Morgan pushed the wrong button. The hull's outer lights turned off.

Spike dragged Morgan's hand across to the correct panel and dropped it.

The Spear's under thrusters blew, tipping the ship ass over teakettle.

The second blast went wide.

"Hit that bleeping ship!" came roaring from the fake cruiser. Frankie, gripping her seat's armrests and trying not to throw up,

Cargo Trouble

had time to think how strange it was that Peters had put child-safety controls on the comms system.

Another voice broke in. "Aggressive cruiser: Identify yourself." Galactic Patrol. It really was as fast as advertised.

But not fast enough. The third blast sliced along the length of the two bigger bulbs of the Sphere.

They went into the jump-tunnel ass-first, bleeding air.

Chapter Eighteen

The Spear came out of the tunnel tumbling.

Frankie did what she could with the two sets of thrusters that still worked, and managed to slow their roll. As soon as she caught her balance, she dropped the seat's safety straps. They had to get the hulls sealed.

"Stay," Morgan said, already up. "We need you here, keeping us steady. Tell me where to go."

"Biggest rip is in the cargo hold."

"Elvin here. I have the materials and am heading there now."

"Excellent, thank you. Second biggest is below us. Down the near stairs and listen for the hissing." Frankie pulled the cord on a trap door in the ceiling, and a cascade of patching materials and glues came down. "Take as much as you can carry. I'm calling the bots up to bring you more. Elvin, you too." She picked up one of the emergency breathers. As Morgan bent to scoop up materials, she pulled it over his head. She put another on herself, and a third for the cat.

As he left, she leaned over to palm the door shut, and then reconsidered. She sat back up.

The cat didn't look any worse for wear. Tufty and disreputable, but that was normal. Frankie didn't know how she had known how to help, but she had. "Spike, you clever girl. Would you run down the halls and close all our doors? Keep their air on the inside."

Spike leapt for the door, easily avoiding Frankie's reach. No breather, then. Frankie could have sworn it said, "sure." But that thought was quickly subsumed by the necessity of explaining simple hull fixes to Morgan, trying to balance the blasters against the torque of the air spilling in four places, and repeatedly assuring Dyad Tunnel Authority that yes, they were moving out of the lane right now.

By the time she got the ship evened out—only a little looseness in the yaw, like a giant drunk fish—Elvin and the box bots had the cargo breach patched. She felt secure enough to join Morgan among the water tanks and pipes and heating. She kept her scan-screens up.

Morgan made up for his lack of knowledge with an overabundance of energy. "I'm all adrenaline!" he said when he saw her. He was soaked, but the burst pipe had been spray-glued shut. The water at their ankles wasn't getting any higher.

Frankie checked her scans. "Water pressure normal. I don't see any more breaks." She looked at him. Droplets in his hair glowed golden in the orange emergency lights. "But we should keep main lights off."

"Agree completely! What's next?"

Frankie frowned at him. "You should go get dry clothes."

"No time! It's hot in here anyway. Why is it so warm in here, anyway?"

Frankie explained how water systems in space vehicles worked

Cargo Trouble

while they walked the length of the capsule. It looked like just the very edge of the scatter-beam had hit them; most of the damage was in parallel streaks and even in the center none of it went deep. Two bulkheads needed to be sealed off, but only one section of the inner hull needed an entire panel patch.

It could have been so much worse.

A long shift later, the Spear wasn't hemorrhaging air anywhere. Morgan and Frankie collapsed in the kitchen nook with warm porridge and cold beer. Spike, who had stayed out of the water and out of everyone's hair, got an entire serving of reconstituted meat product and gravy.

And Elvin appeared. He bowed to her from the kitchen entry. "Permission to board, captain?"

Frankie waved him in. "Glad to see you, Doc." He must have borrowed some of Morgan's overalls; the cuffs looked like they'd been rolled three times. He unhooked a chair from the floor and brought it over, sitting straight while the two of them could barely sit upright on their cushions, even with the support of the back of the bench.

"About our destination," Elvin said, looking at her as if he wanted to splint her posture to the correct angle. "What is it?"

"Short term, we stay wobbling here on this side of the tunnel. Wait for news to come through. Comm links are free so long as we stay in a certain range."

"What news are you expecting?"

"I want to make sure our credits are still good. I would love to hear that that Skoll ship was apprehended, or at least detained."

Morgan frowned. "Won't that make us easy to find? Assuming the Skoll pay off the patrol. Or, more likely, have a second ship."

Frankie waved that problem away. Her balance was off. One beer was one too many. "I lied on the jump application. Everyone thinks we went to Rosings."

Morgan's face lit up as if she'd given him a priceless gift. "Brilliant! Then we'll go home. I mean the home planet in this system. Actually, it's a moon."

Then he frowned. "But once they know we didn't head to Rosing, won't they drone-bomb all the tunnels, looking for us?"

"That is a problem for tomorrow." Frankie lifted her bottle of beer. It was empty. Morgan pushed himself to his feet and got two more. Elvin picked up the empties and took them to the cycler. Frankie followed his path. How was she going to keep track of how many beers she'd had when the bottles disappeared like that?

"And how far is this moon?" she said. "On slow speed with fewest turns."

Morgan sat and pushed a beer her way. He started to write figures on the tabletop with his finger. "About a week, which isn't bad. Not great—we're already out of beer. But," he glanced up at her, "we might get a tow. I know the best collision shop in the sector."

She pushed the beer to Elvin. "Why am I not surprised?"

"Morgan has had his license suspended," Elvin said, pushing the beer back to Morgan. "Twice."

Morgan glared at him. "Thank you, Doctor Elvin."

Elvin shrugged. "Best to have all the data, up front."

Morgan returned to the subject. "My guy, he'll do you up good. And he takes all types of insurance."

Frankie gasped. She'd filled out the forms to get collision insurance, waiting on Morgan's payment. But she never actually sent them in.

She'd be in the red, again.

Way red.

Cargo Trouble

She hoisted herself off the bench. "I'm going to bed."

"Captain, don't you want to weigh in on our destination?" Elvin's voice was simultaneously solicitous and cutting.

Frankie walked past him, lifting her hand to wave the question away. "You know, this past week, I've taken a lot of risks. And a lot of damage."

"So for now, I'm going to go lie down on my own bed with the door closed.

"And repent."

Chapter Nineteen

Frankie started her day on the below deck, vacuuming up the spilled pipe water. At least it hadn't been a sewage pipe. The surface glistened yellow in the orange emergency lights. Safer to keep the main lights off until the mechanics could look at the circuit. The reclamation tank was going to be full, the filters busy, but the system could handle it. She couldn't get to the two closed-off sections. It would be ice in there anyway.

She tried not to hear the tiny, high-pitched drip, drip from somewhere. She'd already looked for it once. It could wait until they got to base. Or moon, or wherever.

She was going to have to ask for terms from the repair shop. Maybe they would agree to hold the ship as collateral while she worked to get the credits to pay for the repairs. But some places charged a fee to store vessels. That would add up fast. Maybe she could get the Spear space worthy, not for travel but for parking in orbit around some lifeless moon while she saved up to pay for the bigger repairs. But she'd have to figure out how to make it more secure than just a wrist-chip lock.

She was nearly done, the floor merely silty, when she heard Morgan coming down the stairs. He wore work overalls that fit him perfectly. He seemed to be talking to someone, but when he came into view he was alone.

"You're right," he said. "Thanks."

"Who are you talking to?"

He waved up the stairs. "Spike. She told me where you were." The cat came into view, giant on the narrow emergency steps. She stopped high above the messy floor and started to clean her paw.

Morgan grabbed the mud scraper and started pushing the fine coating of gunk into a neat row. Frankie was glad to let him.

"Spike talked to you, too?" she said.

Morgan shot her a look. "No," he said slowly. "I asked her where you were, and she trotted over to the stairs. I figured it out from there."

Right. Of course. She'd imagined it. Maybe it was the adrenaline.

"I can't believe she bit me, though." He held his hand up. "Look."

Morgan leaned in. "Didn't break skin. You'll be fine."

He started pushing silt again. "It shouldn't be in her programming."

"She's a cat. Of course it's in her programming."

He looked about to argue, but stopped himself. "Watch out. She's taken over your chair on the bridge. Might be a coup in progress."

Frankie folded up the vacuum and set it on top of her helper bot. "Supply closet B, please. Why did you want to see me, again?"

"Right!" He grinned at her. "Guess what? We're dead!"

He wasn't making any sense. Her arms, suddenly free after having held the vacuum for the past few hours, definitely did not feel dead. "Pardon me?"

Cargo Trouble

"Official story is we went into the tunnel at the wrong angle."

"We did not!"

"Stand down, expert pilot captain ma'am. Nobody blames you. We were being shot at, remember? By a cruiser falsely identifying itself as a Galactic. The cruiser and its commander are currently being detained. Indefinitely."

That part sounded good. Skoll Shipping couldn't have so many cruisers that they'd waste inventory to send another after them. She hoped.

Morgan kept looking at her expectantly, between pushes. What did he want her to say? The news was wrong.

"Captain." He drew the word out as if she were a slow student. "We're dead to the universe. What if we just stayed dead?"

His definition of death must be different from hers. "You mean..."

"Ditch the ship! Or rename it. Give ourselves new names, new IDs." He waited for the other helper bot to position the trash bag in front of the pile he'd made. "Push our old selves into the trash," he said, illustrating. "Tie it up and start over."

"Think about it, Frankie! Captain Styles. Stop running from whatever it is you're running from. Give the Skolls the slip. Be free!"

People did sometimes disappear and then reappear at the edges of Cooperative space. Refugees from a transit disaster, or a seed-planet project everybody had forgotten about.

Frankie thought she knew how to fry the ID chip in her wrist. That would disconnect her from her wristcom, practically disappearing her all by itself.

Who could she be? An astroarcheaologist, like her mom? She'd have to forge credentials. Or go back to school. How much more fun school would be this time if she had a different name. She could fail a course. Join a team. Go out dancing all night.

The Cooperative would be glad she was gone. Win-win.

But Beth would be devastated. And the others. So many of their group had died already. She couldn't do that to them.

Morgan and the bot had finished their mud collection. He bounced on his toes.

"So?"

She had to make him see. "What about your family? Your friends?"

"They'll never have to be disappointed in me again. My father even said 'gravely disappointed' the last time I saw him. How did he know?" His grin wobbled.

She didn't believe him. "They would miss you immensely. And you would never see them again. You couldn't risk it."

His face fell. "It's a trade-off, yes. But it solves all our problems. Debts cleared, slate wiped, future shining bright." He must have been able to tell she was going to say no.

"Frankie," he took her arm gently. "You could be whoever you were meant to be, before the bad stuff happened."

She jerked away from him. That wasn't possible. The Cooperative had seen to that. She would not give them one bit more of herself.

"No," she said. "I'm not running."

She might not be ready to shout her name from the top of CapCities Tower, but she certainly wasn't going to burn it to ash.

"I'm not letting the Skolls—or anybody—take my name away from me."

Chapter Twenty

By the time Frankie had sent all the free messages to all the relevant people and institutions, confirming that yes, she was indeed still alive, the tug from the repair shop had arrived. Morgan must truly be a good repeat customer: The shop didn't even ask for a deposit.

Eckberg Ship Rebuilding sat on the larger of a close pair of terraformed moons circling the twin stars of the Dyad System. In only half a day, they could see it coming into view.

More brown than blue, swirling with clouds, and packed with buildings and transit tubes, the moon looked happily prosperous, at least from space. Frankie chose to tie off at their orbital platform, just a few slips and a very chipper mechanic inspector. The inspector, a somewhat ruddy young person, sent her big drones around the outer hull and walked with the smaller ones through the Spear, starting far aft, in the cargo sphere.

"Big ship," she said. "Gonna take a while." After that, she pointedly ignored Frankie. Another spacer who obviously liked to work alone.

Frankie was halfway down the walkway back to the main sphere when she saw Morgan, leaning on the railing and staring down at his container. She stopped beside him and matched his position. "You're worried she's going to scan the stables?"

"No. A redhead, right? If she's who I think she is, her mom built the stable. No worries there." He shrugged at her surprise. "Home system, remember?"

He didn't seem that happy about it. Mouth turned down, arms all floppy, cuffs mussed.

Frankie changed the subject, as much as she could. She called up a map screen and homed in on Dyad system. "How can I help you get the container moved? Where is its final destination?"

His laugh tasted bitter. "You've done a bang-up job with that. Sorry about the pun, couldn't help it. The stable is housed here." On the map, he pointed to the second moon.

"Like I said. Home."

"Cloud," she read. "You're named for your moon?"

"It's my middle name, if you must know. And I guess you must, now that we're here."

"Here where?"

He looked directly at her. "You don't know this place?"

She shrugged. "Wasn't on my route. I don't know a lot about the outer sectors." She pinched the moon bigger. Looked like any other new terraform project. Not a lot of buildings yet. They must have started with the other moon, Silva. Forest. "Looks like they got the names switched. Cloud should be the big one."

A message blinked across her screen. The insurance company? She swiped it open, and gasped.

"Did you do this?" She looked at Morgan and pointed to the part of the message that said, "Fully Covered."

Morgan scanned the note, and shook his head no. "Guess Past Captain Frankie was looking out for you." She frowned at him.

"Maybe you did it in your sleep?" He shrugged.

She swept the screen to the side and called up her main credit account. "It's all still there. Wasn't me."

"Maybe you just haven't paid the premium yet."

Seriously? He'd never had to pay an insurance premium? She glared at him.

But it was clear he was deep in his own thoughts.

Morgan pushed up from his slouch. "Listen, Frankie. Captain. It's going to take a while before your ship is patched-up. Why don't you come to Cloud with me? Cheaper than a hotel."

"Not a chance."

"Why not? It's beautiful. Bucolic and peaceful."

"Bucolic maybe. Peaceful I am sure it's not." She poked him, gently, but in no-G it set him back on his grav-booted heels. "You are obviously the black sheep of your family. When was the last time you were here?"

He looked sheepish. "Four years."

"Right. Your family, do they know you're here?" He shook his head. "As soon as they do, you know they're going to be all over you. You want a distraction. I will not be that distraction." It was bad enough not having a family of her own. She was not going to suffer through the tempests of some stranger's family.

"It would be a blast. You could eat peppermints by the handful and watch the fireworks."

She crossed her arms. "No."

He sighed. "Worth a shot. Hey," he said as she started heading to the airlock. "What if I stay with you instead?"

She snorted. "I'm staying on the ship." No use spending money on some random bed when she had twelve perfectly nice ones. "But you might send me some of those peppermints." She kicked the panel to open the door and passed through, Morgan hard on her heels.

He followed her all the way to the kitchen. Thoughts of peppermint had reminded Frankie she hadn't eaten yet today. She rehydrated two ProntoPestos. He hovered as they cooked, helping get the water bottles and set the table. She dumped the contents of the steaming packets into two bowls and handed him one. She reclaimed her usual seat, facing the door. The cat, wherever it was, could claim a different perch.

Morgan let her eat in peace, at least. As soon as she was finished, a full ten minutes after he'd done wolfing his portion, he took in a breath.

She held up a hand. "No. Final."

He blew the breath out, defeated. "Fine," he said. "When do you want me off? Oh-sixteen-thirty-two?"

That wasn't even a time, and he knew it. "Why are you so mad? Just catch a shuttle and go back to Smithson. Or Rosing. Or anywhere else."

"My mom would die if she found out I'd been so close and not come by. My dad would kill me."

Their voices must have attracted Spike. The cat, even raggedier-looking than before, sat just inside the door and stared at her.

"You want a cat?" she asked Morgan.

"Not that one," he said.

Frankie looked over to Spike's dining area. Half a gravy-thingy remained. The water bowl was fine, too. "What?" she said to the cat.

Spike gazed at her steadily. She was not going to get into a staring match with a cat. Spike closed her eyes slowly, and then opened them, slowly. Frankie shrugged, clueless. Spike sighed and headed out the door. She turned, tilted her head toward the end of the hall with the piloting room, and left in that direction.

"I believe I'm being summoned," Frankie said. She rose, reaching for the empty bowls.

Cargo Trouble

"I'll get this," Morgan said, still sullen. "It's the least I can do."

Frankie was starting to remember why she didn't like people like him. "Don't just run away. Say goodbye before you go."

"Goodbye, then," he said, facing the kitchen disposal and away from her.

Chapter Twenty-One

Spike sat on the communications console, her tail waving side to side.

Frankie looked around the room, messy with burst patch-kits and used drink pouches. The arms of the comms chair were sticky. What had Morgan eaten in here? The consoles, on the other hand, were unusually dark and quiet. Screens off, engine off, solar sails out, no port chatter. Readings shunted to her comm screen.

She grabbed a wipe from the nearest patch-kit and cleaned her hands and then the arms of the chair. Spike waited, tail still slowly wagging. She sat on the now-clean chair and folded her hands in her lap. They gazed at each other.

Enough of that. Frankie raised her eyebrows. "You wanted something?"

Spike pounced on the call button. The connection came nearly instantaneously. A masculine-presenting person she didn't recognize appeared on the screen.

"Captain Styles. It's nice to finally meet you." He pronounced her name correctly—Stee-lay. She'd never heard anyone not from her home planet who said it that way. It sounded strange, after all this time.

"Sir." She guessed at the pronoun.

"Let's call me Bruce." He had a dark square face made more square by thick black hair that ended evenly with equally thick sideburns, connected by a sharply trimmed moustache. "I represent a firm that hires people like you to find ... things."

She frowned. People like who? What things? "You mean, information?"

"Sometimes. Sometimes actual things. Or people." He chuckled, smoothing out his perfect moustache. "This must all sound rather mysterious." He shrugged. "Can't be helped."

She didn't answer.

"Captain, we've had our eye on you for a long time. Since university, in fact."

"You know who I am, then?"

"Yes, but it doesn't matter to us."

Frankie sat straight. "It doesn't?"

"We were delighted that you chose this line of work, and we will pay you to continue doing it. On top of that, we ask that you carry out occasional information-gathering assignments for us. Bonuses apply."

Frankie shook her head. "This is all very deus ex machina of you."

"The timing is coincidental. My agent had already started observing you before your little adventure. Closely observing. She's there with you now."

"Spike?" Frankie's gaze, horrified, shot to the cat, or whatever it was. It walked into the camera's field, and nodded at Bruce.

A secret agent had cuddled with her.

She'd slept with it!

Cargo Trouble

"Unfortunate name, but she got it when she was little, and she likes it."

Spike tilted her head askance at Bruce, then started cleaning her shoulder.

They were getting off-topic. "Let me get this straight," Frankie said. "You work for a private company—"

"—Public-private partnership—"

"—that will pay me to ship cargo and also to ... what? Hunt for clues? Spy?"

"On-site research." Bruce's sideburns moved apart when he smiled. His teeth were very white. "A recent assignment was to locate the mother of a little girl who ran away and then forgot her family name. Another was to determine if a certain family remained in possession of a certain artwork they had claimed stolen."

"Like solving puzzles. People puzzles."

"The best kind! "What do you say?"

She didn't have to say yes now. She could say no.

"There's a contract?"

Bruce looked down. "Sending it. Standard, for this kind of work."

The contract was relatively simple. A base income in the range of the second-to-top tier of the dockmasters' scale. Per-diem for the length of each special assignment, plus expenses. Guaranteed two assignments per year, 20 days minimum, paid even if unused.

One addendum: A nondisclosure agreement.

What was the catch?

Frankie looked up. "Tell me more about your company."

"Systems Analysis. Address on the contract. I'll wait for you to look it up."

It came up first in the search results, despite the mundane name. "Philanthropic venture funders. Truly?"

"Cross my heart."

"Based on Rosing Station." Her hopes fell. "I can't go to Rosing."

"But wait. As a signing incentive, I've already managed your Skoll problem."

"It wasn't my problem." Well, except for the aiding and abetting.

"And that made it easier to manage the family, believe you me. But I do think we took care of the young man's debt as well. That part of the discussion was a little ... opaque." For the first time, Bruce looked less than confident. It made her trust him more.

She'd lost her shipping contract, and this one could replace it. She would keep helping people not starve, and maybe reunite families. She loved solving puzzles.

She didn't want to lose her freedom.

"Sounds interesting," she said. "The Spear would need better shielding, and upgraded communications."

"Done. I'll tell Eckberg."

"And a ship-to-satellite credit account?"

"We'll see."

She smiled. So they did have limits. "Second-to-last thing. Can we agree to a six-month trial period? Six months, either party out, no foul."

Bruce had to lean out of camera range on that one. He leaned back in. "We'll get that out to you, soon as Scott is back from lunch. Last thing?"

"Is Spike assigned to me, or is she off to the next recruit?"

"For the six-month trial, she'll be with you. Barring unforeseen events." Spike perked up at that news, pushing her way on-camera again. "Think of it as a vacation," Bruce said to her, flashing another bright smile.

Cargo Trouble

"We took fire." A simulated voice growled out of the fur at Spike's neck.

Frankie kicked the chair away from the console. The chair, bolted to the deck, did not move. Frankie swallowed her shout of pain.

"I read the report." Bruce's smile vanished. "It shouldn't have gone that far."

"My fault? No. Absolutely no." Spike's tale whipped side to side. Frankie leaned as far away from it as she could.

"You weren't the only agent there."

"Talk to the union rep," Spike spat. She jumped off the console and stalked out of the room, only pausing to kick the door shut with a hind leg.

"Spike is one of our best in the field, Captain. But, as is often true with a diva, she has a few sharp edges. You'll work out fine."

Frankie turned back to Bruce, and caught him wiping his brow with a bandana. "Is Spike really a cat? Some special kind?"

"Spike is her own being. She will share her story in her own good time. So, captain," Bruce's smile was back. "Can we count on you?"

She'd traded a snake for some fancy secret-agent cat. She'd get her ship upgraded for free. She'd have guaranteed income for half a year, at least.

No need to say no.

"Deal."

"Fantastic. Here's your first assignment: You're off duty until Spear is whole again. Get yourself down to Silva and have a little fun. Expense it to Systems. Scott will show you how."

"Welcome to the team, Captain Styles."

The call cut off with a pop. Frankie leaned back in the chair, winded after doing nothing but sitting and talking. Systems Bruce was right. She did need some time off.

She pulled up a screen to see what sort of adventures Silva promised.

Also by Nicky Penttila

Cooperative Realm: Arkhide

Secrets of the Synths

Worlds Apart

Hidden Planet

The Listeners

The Elders of Arkhide

Cooperative Realm: Frankie

Cargo Trouble

Frankie Takes a Holiday

Frankie Takes a Dive

Historical Fiction

A Note of Scandal

An Untitled Lady

The Spanish Patriot

About the Author

Nicky Penttila wrote her first story, a Mayan murder mystery, in seventh grade. But then came gymnastics, math team, and boyfriends. Later came husband, car payments, and a sleep-depriving work schedule at newspapers across the country. Then came a second career as a science writer. But the fiction kept trickling out, a story here, a novella there, and finally, a real live novel. And she hasn't stopped.

Find more great reads at nickypenttila.com

Made in the USA
Middletown, DE
16 October 2024